THE POWER
OF BLOOD

Sami Youssef

For the ruthless immortal cosmos

CONTENTS

THE AWAKENING

Part One

The Power
of Blood

By

Sami Youssef

CHAPTER 1

The Divided City

Tare'Envel's skyline loomed high, a jagged silhouette carved against the dim light of the overcast sky. A city of vast distinction, where the polished stones of the High City gleamed with the wealth and power of the elite, while the crumbling streets of the Undercity lay in perpetual shadow—clinging to life through desperation and cunning.

The air was thick with the mingling scents of smoke, sweat, and blood, a grim concoction that barely masked the rot and decay seeping from the city's underbelly. Here survival wasn't just a skill, it was an art, and Kestus 'Quickhand' Retchet was an artist.

Perched atop a crumbling rooftop, Kestus surveyed the chaotic patchwork of life below. The streets twisted and coiled like a living maze, illuminated only by the flickering, uneven glow of rusted oil lamps. Shadows danced on every surface, stretching long and thin, masking faces and deeds alike.

The rhythmic hum of the Undercity pulsed beneath him: gangs staking claims, traders haggling over stolen goods, and the weak clinging desperately to whatever scraps they could guard. This was the true city—the one built on grit, fear, and stolen moments of triumph.

From this vantage point, Kestus could see it all. And yet, he felt as invisible as the wind.

That was how he preferred it.

He was neither highborn nor bound by blood to any gang; he was a man who lived and moved outside the Undercity's unspoken rules. To some, he was a phantom—a ghost who slipped through the cracks —leaving no trace behind.

His name, Quickhand, wasn't just a boast. It was a warning. Kestus had a knack of making impossible jobs possible.

His eyes shifted westward, where the Starstride gang held sway over the bustling market district. His tattered cloak swayed with the night's breeze as he observed the vibrant, chaotic life below. Even at this late hour, the district thrummed with energy —merchants bargaining over their wares, laborers hurrying about their business, and Starstride enforcers keeping a watchful presence from atop balconies or patrolling the crowded streets.

The Starstride were unlike the common thugs that populated the Undercity. Under Tyven the Blade's leadership, they had evolved into something closer to a shadowed guild than a street gang. Tyven had instilled a code of conduct that brought a tenuous peace to the district—a peace paid for in blood, but peace nonetheless.

Kestus respected Tyven's operation. The man had a sense of honor, a trait as rare in the Undercity as sunlight. However, that honor came with a price: if you fell into Tyven's debt, you owed him, and he always collected.

Kestus preferred to remain unshackled, untouched by any gang's claim. Freedom was his currency, and he had no intention of trading it for anything.

Still Starstride wasn't the only power vying for control of Tare'Envel's shadowy streets.

To the east, near the docks and black markets, the Knife Point gang reigned with an iron grip and a thirst for trouble. Where Starstride valued order, Knife Point revered brutality. Their leader, Darron Ironfist, was a man without conscience or restraint. Under his rule, Knife Point had become a force of unchecked violence, their name spoken in quiet tones of terror.

Kestus had crossed paths with Knife Point thugs

before, each encounter a narrow escape before bloodshed ensued. Their methods left scars— not on Kestus himself, but on the streets they terrorized. The people under their thumb lived in perpetual fear, never knowing when the gang might descend upon them to take what little they had—or worse. For Knife Point, it wasn't just about wealth or territory, it was about dominance. Refuse to join them and you could become another victim, another warning to the rest.

Then there was RavenHood—a far smaller gang, with a reputation that rivaled the largest. They were currently led by Filko Sharp-Eye, a man of great intelligence and an even greater grace. RavenHood did not rely on brute strength or numbers. Their power came from precision, stealth, and secrecy. They thrived in the realm of shadows; their expertise lying in assassinations, espionage, and high-stakes thefts. RavenHood had no interest in ruling the streets or intimidating the weak. They moved like whispers in the darkness, unseen until it was far too late.

Kestus had always admired their craft. He wasn't in the game for power or bloodshed. He was in it for the thrill—the artistry of the heist. In many ways, he shared their philosophy. Yet, even RavenHood paled in comparison to the newest gang.

The Hushed.

No one truly understood them, nor did anyone want to. No one knew who led them or how many there were. They were specters, their influence spreading like a plague through the Undercity. Stories of dark rituals and eldritch power clung to their name like a shroud. It was said they could vanish into thin air, or drive men to madness with nothing more than a glance.

The most chilling of all, however, was said to be their veil. It was believed that if you were to see a Hushed unveil themselves, it would be as if you were staring into the very face of death.

Kestus had never encountered the Hushed directly —and he had no intention of changing that. Their power wasn't measured in coin or territory. It was measured in fear.

Drawing in a slow, deliberate breath, Kestus let the cool night air fill his lungs. The Undercity was a fragile web, each gang playing its part in an uneasy balance. For years, Kestus had danced between their territories, careful to avoid alliances and vendettas alike.

Except tonight, the air felt different. There was a tension that clung to the streets, a palpable unease, as if the city itself was holding its breath.

Something was coming.

Slipping down a crumbling stairwell into the alley

below, Kestus descended from his rooftop perch with practiced ease. His boots barely whispered against the cobblestones as he moved, his dark and tattered cloak wrapped tightly around him to ward off both the cold and curious eyes. Head low, he melted into the shadows, making his way through the winding streets toward his destination.

It lay at the edge of Starstride's territory: a small, unassuming tavern called the Dry Spell. A rare gem in the Undercity—a place of neutrality, where deals were made, secrets were traded, and men like Kestus could meet without worrying about a dagger in their back.

CHAPTER 2

The Dry Spell

The tavern was dimly lit, filled with the low murmur of half-heard conversations and the thick haze of pipe smoke. The walls bore the scars of countless brawls, their wood darkened and warped from years of neglect.

It was a place where deals were struck in whispers and betrayals were sealed with handshakes.

Kestus stepped through the door, his trained eyes scanning the room with ease.

It didn't take long to spot Jeret. The grizzled man was seated in the far corner, half-hidden by shadows, his posture relaxed yet still alert. The dim glow of a single lantern reflected off his glass, the liquid within catching the light as he swirled it idly. Kestus left his hood up as he moved toward the man, his steps quiet and deliberate.

Jeret was a Starstrider, a blood-sworn member of the gang. He wasn't one of the brutish enforcers who patrolled the market with clubs in hand and scars to prove their mettle. He operated in the shadows. Jeret was a named man. They called him Jeret the Smile. He dealt in information, arranged jobs, and kept his ear to the pulse of Tare'Envel's underbelly.

Kestus had worked with Jeret before. In a city where trust was a foreign concept, Jeret was as close to reliable as one could hope for. Still, Kestus kept his guard up.

Sliding into the seat opposite Jeret, Kestus said nothing, his expression unreadable beneath the shadow of his hood. Jeret glanced up from his drink, that thin, ever-present smile plastered across his face.

"You going to take that hood off, Kestus Retchet?" Jeret asked, his voice low and smooth, like the liquor he swirled. "Wearing them indoors is mighty suspicious. People might get the wrong idea."

Kestus ignored the prod.

"Glad you showed," Jeret continued, leaning back in his chair. "Wasn't sure you'd take the risk. There's already a lot of buzz about this one."

"I'm here," Kestus replied, his tone flat. "Let's hear it, Smile."

Jeret's smile widened, though his eyes gleamed with something sharper, more calculating.

"Straight to business. I always like that." He leaned forward, resting his elbows on the table. "There's an offer. A job."

Kestus raised an eyebrow. "That's nothing new."

"This one's different." Jeret shook his head, his smile dropping a bit. "It's not just a job—it's THE job. A heist, to be precise."

"Go on." Kestus leaned in slightly despite himself. Curiosity tugged at him, though he kept his expression neutral.

"This could change everything." Jeret's voice was barely above a whisper now. He gestured with his glass, the amber liquid inside sloshing slightly. "There's an artifact. A bracer, to be exact." With a quick swig, Jeret winced. "Ever heard of the Shiftscape Bracer?"

Kestus' brow furrowed. He'd heard the name before, whispered in passing—rumors of a relic with powers far beyond understanding. Stories like that were common in Tare'Envel, though most were nothing more than drunken fantasies or children's tales.

"Who hasn't heard of the Shiftscape Bracer?"

Jeret leaned back, his teeth flashing in the dim light.

"True everyone's heard stories but, now we know the bracer's feckin real. And not only that. It's in King Alikhan's castle, locked away in his private vault."

Mind racing, Kestus drummed his fingers against the table.

"You're asking me to infiltrate the High City, break into the castle, find the King's private vault, all just to steal a bracelet?" His tone was calm, and yet the enormity of the task was clear in his words.

Jeret nodded, his grin never faltering. "Not just me, my friend. Starstride wants this. Tyven himself is backing the job. He even hired some RavenHood to gather the intel."

The mention of Tyven and RavenHood gave Kestus pause. This was a big one for sure. The leader of Starstride wasn't a man who acted on whims. If Tyven wanted the bracer badly enough to risk angering King Alikhan the Stern, there had to be more to this job than Jeret was letting on.

"If it's real, the stories can't be true. So, what makes this bracer so special?" Kestus asked, his fingers stilling as he leaned in.

Jeret leaned in closer. "They say all the rumors of the Shiftscape are true. This bracer—it is true magic. The kind of thing that could turn the tides of power in Tare'Envel. With that kind of leverage, even the King wouldn't be untouchable. Undercity could rise up. That is…if a thief can get it from him before he uses it."

Kestus closed his eyes, his mind churning. Artifacts like that—if they were real—came with a price. Not just the risk of stealing them, it was the consequences of possessing them. In Tare'Envel, power like that didn't just change hands. It left bodies in its wake.

"Let's say I deliver the bracer, you really trust Tyven with something like this?" Kestus asked, his tone edged with skepticism.

"Trust?" Jeret chuckled, the sound low and gravelly. "No one trusts anybody. But if I trusted someone it would be the Blade. Look, you don't know the man. I know Tyven has a plan, and this bracer is the key to it. If you don't trust him, trust he won't shite on the Undercity."

Kestus sat back, crossing his arms. "And you think I'm the right thief to pull this off?"

"You're the only one who can." Jeret's grin widened, his eyes gleaming.

Showing a smile of his own, Kestus tilted his head toward Jeret. "Let's say I believe—you believe that. What's the catch, Smile? There's more to this."

Jeret's eyes grew sober and circled the table. Kestus could see he was reluctant to share too much.

"I don't know all the details," he admitted, his fingers fluttering above his glass like nervous birds. "But there are whispers…" His voice dropped even lower.

Suddenly, Jeret's cup tipped, falling to its side. The remnants of his barrel-aged liquor spilling into the cracks of the table, glistening like liquid amber in the dim light. The cup began to roll toward the edge. In an instant Jeret's features grew solemn, as if he were receiving a bad omen. Then just before the cup fell, Kestus' hand darted out, catching it in one swift motion.

The action brought a smile back to Jeret's face. "Quickhand." He nodded to himself. "The Hushed."

The words sent a chill down Kestus' spine. His back stiffened, his gaze darting between Jeret and the mess on the table, searching for his response in the worn woodgrain.

"They've been seen near the castle," Jeret continued, his voice even. "I don't know what they're after. We just know they're involved. Some intel says they're working with Alikhan. Others think they're after the bracer themselves. And a few…" He paused, swallowing the lump in his throat. "A few say they're looking for new recruits. Whatever the truth is, it's more than just the King's guard on the lookout."

The Hushed. Kestus struggled to steady his thoughts. He'd heard enough stories to know that if the Hushed were involved, this wasn't just dangerous—it was a gamble with death itself.

Kestus tapped his fingers against the table, weighing the risks in his mind.

A heist like this would put him squarely in the crosshairs of every gang and guard in Tare'Envel. The Hushed, the King's forces, and even Starstride would all have a stake in the outcome. However, if the bracer was truly as valuable as Jeret suggested, the reward might outweigh the danger.

"Why me?" Kestus asked, breaking the silence. "You've got plenty of thieves in Starstride who could get into the castle. Tyven has already involved RavenHood on the mapping, why not pay for the full job? This sounds like another legendary tale for Talons. What makes me so unique?"

Jeret leaned back in his chair, crossing his arms. His calculating expression returned.

"Because you're not one of Starstride or RavenHood," he admitted, his voice casual. "You've got a reputation in the Undercity—you're a named man. You can get into places others find impossible. Before long, you'll be as infamous as Talons even. However, you're not tied to any gang. You're an outsider, everywhere you go. That makes you...

expendable."

Kestus let out a sound halfway between a grunt and a laugh. "Good to know I'm valued."

"It's not personal." Jeret shrugged, unfazed. "Tyven doesn't want to risk one of his own if this goes south. If King Alikhan knew Starstride was involved he would probably use the Crimson Guard to hunt the gangs down, and Tyven is trying to avoid that. They have a history. Not only that but with the Hushed involved, this isn't just about a payout anymore—it's about survival. That's where you come in. You've got the skills, and you're good at keeping your head down. Do what you do, get in and get out. They won't suspect us if a master thief gets the job done right."

Kestus leaned forward, his fingers tapping faster. The stakes were higher than he'd expected. Tyven wouldn't back something he didn't think was possible, though. Hiring RavenHood and an independent contractor made sense after hearing everything Jeret had to say.

Still, the Hushed.

They weren't just another gang. They were something else entirely—more like a cult than criminals. Kestus had heard the stories: of men driven mad after crossing paths with them, of others disappearing without a trace. Their members were said to wield dark, unnatural powers. Whatever their goals were, they inspired a fear few dared to speak of.

Nevertheless, the job was tempting. High-stakes challenges like this were what Kestus lived for. And if he could gain Tyven's favor, there were potential advantages beyond the bracer.

Is it worth the risk?

After a long pause, Kestus looked up at Jeret from beneath his hood. "I'll need everything in advance. Plans, schematics, everything."

Jeret nodded, the glint of anticipation returning to his eyes. "We've got it all. Map to the vault, guard routines, you name it. Tyven hired a RavenHood spy to infiltrate the castle, and I'll be stationed with a group of Striders to watch for any cutthroats who might try to interfere." He leaned closer, lowering his voice further. "The window is tight, Quickhand. Intel says the artifact is being moved in a span of days. Once it's gone, the opportunity's gone with it. We need to move fast."

Kestus stood, his movements deliberate. "Thanks, Smile. I'll tell you my answer tomorrow night."

"What?!" Jeret nearly toppled from his chair, his voice rising before he caught himself. A few heads turned their way, and he hastily coughed into his fist, feigning nonchalance. Rising to his feet with forced composure, he turned his back to the curious gazes of the tavern's patrons.

"Dammit, Quickhand," Jeret whispered, his frustration barely contained. "Fine. We can spare a day. Meet me at the usual spot tomorrow. Midnight. You say yes, we move forward. You say no, and I'll find a real thief who can handle a real job."

Kestus nodded, a faint smile flickering beneath his hood. "Until then, Smile."

Without another word, he turned and slipped out of the tavern.

The cool night air struck his face as he stepped into the streets of the Undercity, pulling his cloak tight around him. In the dim light of spluttering lanterns, Kestus seemed to blend with the shadows, his footsteps soundless on the uneven stone.

His mind churned with thoughts, replaying the conversation, dissecting the risks and rewards.

The Shiftscape Bracer.

Power beyond wealth.

The Hushed.

He moved quickly, weaving through the twisted streets as if carried by memory alone.

The Undercity was quieter now, its usual mania reduced to distant shouts and the occasional clatter of a drunk stumbling through an alley. Kestus preferred the night—it sharpened his focus and gave him space to think.

Instinct kept him from taking the same path twice. Even if no one was following, it was a habit now, a survival skill as ingrained as breathing. Passing through a narrow corridor, he spotted a group of thugs lounging outside a boarded-up shop. Their eyes flicked toward him, sharp and assessing.

Knife Point.

The insignia on their sleeves and the practiced menace in their posture marked them clearly. Kestus kept his pace steady, neither quickening nor slowing. He hadn't crossed into their territory, and they seemed smart enough not to provoke someone without cause. These were seasoned men, not young hotheads looking to prove themselves.

Strange. They don't often lurk so close.

He passed without incident, his focus returning to the path ahead.

Eventually, he reached a small, unassuming building nestled between two larger structures. The door groaned as he pushed it open, releasing a faint scent of old wood and stale parchment.

His hideout.

It was a simple space—a single room with a bed in one corner, shelves lining the walls with tools and supplies, and a table cluttered with maps and notes. It wasn't much, but it had always been enough.

"Maybe it's time for something more," Kestus wondered aloud, the thought catching him off guard.

The room seemed smaller than usual tonight, its worn edges closing in around him. He lit a small oil lamp, the dim glow illuminating the table. Sitting down in his worn chair, he pulled a sheet of parchment toward him and began sketching a rough map of King Alikhan's castle from memory.

The layout was mostly guesswork. He'd only been to the High City a handful of times, and the castle itself was a fortress in every sense of the word. Its grandeur masked layers of security—both magical and mundane. King Alikhan and his predecessors hadn't spared any effort in ensuring their safety, even from their own subjects.

Jeret had promised more details and schematics that could fill in the gaps, only if Kestus took the job, though.

He couldn't deny it, his interest was piqued.

The High City was a world apart from the Undercity. Gleaming towers, polished stone, and streets lined with gold were its hallmarks. No matter how it looked, however, Kestus knew the truth. Beneath the glimmering facade lay a web of secrets, corruption, and power plays that rivaled anything the gangs of the Undercity could conjure.

He stared at the incomplete map before him, his thoughts swirling. The King's vault was said to be the most secure location in all of Tare'Envel. Breaking into it wasn't just difficult—it was the kind of feat that would become legend.

"This is impossible," he muttered, leaning back in his creaking chair. "No matter how I look at it, I don't know how I can pull it off."

He could get past all the guards, infiltrate the castle, break into the King's vault, and still there would be the Hushed.

That was the part that unnerved him. Their motives were unclear, their methods horrifying. Stories of their unnatural powers and the madness they left in their wake weren't just rumors—they were warnings. If they were involved, failure wasn't an option. And even success might not guarantee survival.

Kestus pushed the map aside along with his thoughts, staring at the ceiling as the lamp's flickering light cast shadows that danced across the walls.

Unable to fight it back, a heavy yawn forced him further back into his chair. The movement of his reflection in a small reflective glass caught his attention. Still in his old and tattered cloak, he noticed the dull color of tiredness in his hazel eyes.

The trio of blue, brown and green mixed with the red of the veins.Trying to wipe it away, he yawned again. This time not fighting it, he ran his hands through his wavy hair and tucked it behind his ears. A wavy curl flipped up at the end of the strand, undoing his effort.

One night to decide. Maybe rest will help.

Removing his cloak, he let it hang from the chair.

You keep working.

He removed his boots and moved to the bed to lay down.

One night to weigh the risks and rewards.

One night to determine whether this was the job that would finally set him up for life—or the one that would end it.

Tomorrow night, he would give Jeret his answer. And whatever that answer was, there would be no turning back.

For the first time in years, Kestus wasn't sure which way the scales would tip.

CHAPTER 3

The Bloated and the Rich

The wind swept through the narrow alleyways of Tare'Envel's Undercity, carrying the scent of sweat, grime, and old stone. Kestus moved swiftly, his steps quiet, each motion calculated to blend into the rhythm of the streets. Jeret's offer weighed heavily on his mind, the lack of sleep hanging from beneath his eyes, and though Kestus had tried to set it aside, it clung to him like a coin turning over and over in his thoughts.

The Shiftscape Bracer. Wealth. Power.
None of it would come easy.

Kestus frowned, slipping down a side alley, navigating the maze of damp narrow passages that made up the Undercity. His instincts told him something wasn't right, to tell Jeret no. The Hushed were involved, and that accounted for something. Kestus had always been confident, however, now it was time to be smart, not cocky. He couldn't let riches and prestige cloud his decision.

That alone should've been enough to make him walk away. Except Kestus had built his reputation on doing the impossible, taking on jobs that others wouldn't touch, and this was no different. There had been other times death was on the line and Kestus was still breathing. It was a challenge—a deadly one, but a challenge nonetheless.

He could still hear Jeret's voice, the way he casually dropped Tyven's interest in all of this.

Tyven has clearly put a lot on the line for this job. Why? What does he want this bracer for? What's his big plan? There's something at play here. I need to know more.

That bothered Kestus more than he wanted to admit. Tyven the Blade was a legend. Few names held as much power as Tyven's inTare'Envel.

The lights of the tavern caught Kestus' attention. He didn't realize he had already arrived. The sign read,

"The Bloated and the Rich."

The only thing bloated was the sign, from the swelling with each rain. And the rich? The drinks were so cheap, it was hard to believe the tavern made any profit. The clientele weren't in much better condition either. Thanks to the traffic, this was a favored spot for those in Kestus' profession, too many faces passing through to remember any one in particular.

Pushing the tavern door open, he was met with the familiar scent of dried ale and wood smoke. It was quieter than usual, only a few patrons scattered throughout, huddled over drinks. That was odd, especially for this hour. Still, Kestus made his way to a dark corner, slipping into a seat, where he could watch the entrance and the crowd without being noticed.

His hands already tapping the table, Kestus pulled them back to his sides. With a quick adjustment, Kestus made sure his hood didn't reveal too many details of his face.
The dark grey cloak, now thin from usage, didn't do much anymore. The pockets had holes, the thread had thinned, it was more likely someone would think him a beggar than Kestus Quickhand —*Master Thief.* It had definitely seen better days.

He hadn't been sitting long when a familiar voice broke through his thoughts.

"I'm glad you showed."

Kestus turned, his eyes locking on Jeret, who grunted as he knelt into the seat across from him. The Starstride member looked as relaxed as ever, a sly grin on his face. Again, Kestus could see the flicker of excitement in the man's brown eyes. He always got like this before a big job, practically buzzing with anticipation.

I haven't even given him an answer yet.

"I said I'd think about it," Kestus replied, keeping his voice low.

"The fact I could get a drink and approach before you even marked me, it is clear you have been really contemplating this." Jeret drank from his pint, revealing an even wider smile as he set his drink atop the table. Cheap beer dampened his mustache and beard. "You being here is all the answer I need."

Kestus hesitated, glancing around the room. The atmosphere was thick with murmurs as more people started to filter in, the clinking of mugs covered their conversation. No one seemed interested in the two men in the corner, even so Kestus knew better than to let his guard down-a second time.

"It's a dangerous play," Kestus admitted after a while. "King Alikhan's castle is a fortress. Security is tighter than it's ever been, I assume the bracer is why. Not only that, you're asking me to go after something that'll have the deadliest gang in the city watching."

Jeret's grin didn't falter. "So you're in."

"The Hushed…"

"The Hushed are always around. Like rats in the walls, always watching but rarely making a move. Knife Point wouldn't get near the place for that same reason. They have no tact or skill. You could hear or smell the brutes before they even made their way into the High City. And RavenHood, they did their part already. If this job is a success, they get a piece of the renown on top of their coin. Got any other worries?"

Kestus leaned in, his expression hardening. "It is more than just a heist."

Jeret's grin softened, his voice lowering to match Kestus'. "You're not wrong. This is more than a heist. That's why Tyven's backing it. The Shiftscape Bracer isn't just some trinket. It has… power, Quickhand. Real power."

"Power? That's what you said last night. What do you mean by power?" Kestus asked, narrowing his eyes.

"Power like the old stories. You know? Old magic." Jeret's gaze grew distant, his voice carrying something dangerous. "No one's entirely sure where the bracer came from. They say it's from the ancient days—back when the gods still meddled in our world. Rumors speak of the Shiftscape Bracer being able to transform or teleport or something crazy like that. Won't know exactly until we get it"

Kestus' gut tightened. He had heard enough legends of the Undercity's buried past, of relics tied to forgotten gods and lost empires. Most of it was nonsense. Except, Kestus knew not all of it was nonsense and the Hushed were living proof that some of those legends had roots in reality. If this bracer was tied to such magic, this job had just become far more dangerous.

"And you didn't think to mention this earlier?" Kestus kept his voice controlled, yet there was an edge to his words.

Jeret raised his hands in mock defense. "Look, I'm telling you what I know. Like you said, I told you this thing had power. It was you who didn't ask. How was I to know what you did or didn't already know?" Jeret softened. "Tyven isn't giving all the details, Quickhand. He's serious about this though. And if Tyven's serious, you know the job's worth it. Pull this off, and you'll be set for life. Protection, wealth, anything you want."

Kestus sat back, considering. The Blade wasn't known for taking unnecessary risks. If he wanted the Shiftscape Bracer, it meant there was something larger at stake than a simple power play between the gangs, and that made Kestus wary.

"This bracer, whatever it is, must be more valuable

to the Hushed than it is to us. Otherwise, they wouldn't be lurking. Not to mention, what if King Alikhan catches wind of this? I assume everyone in the Undercity is talking about it. It's only a matter of time until High City does." Kestus frowned watching his fingers tapping the table. He didn't notice when he started tapping again.

Jeret's grin faltered, only for a moment. "Tyven's confident they won't interfere, as long as we don't provoke them. The Hushed may be involved, but they don't play the same game as the other gangs. They have their own agenda, whatever that may be and if they were opposed to this, they would've already intervened."

"And if we cross their agenda?" Kestus asked.

Jeret's grin vanished. "Then we're dead. Simple as that. Same as if we get caught by King Alikhan. Dead. So, don't get caught. Don't get dead."

Kestus let out a slow breath, considering his options. The offer was more dangerous than anything he'd ever taken on. The potential payoff was enough to set him up for life though. That was, if he survived. Still, this was the kind of challenge he thrived on. He made a name for himself by pulling off the impossible.

Why stop now? *Kestus Quickhand. After this they'll call me something like, Kestus the King's Bane or*

Phantom Fingers.

"I'm in," Kestus said reluctantly.

Jeret's smile returned, wider than before. He reached into his cloak, pulling out a small, rolled-up parchment.

"Here. This has the details—entry points, guards' schedules, the vault's location. We move in two nights."

Kestus took the parchment, slipping it into his pocket. "Two nights."

Jeret rose, chugged down his drink, and clapped Kestus on the shoulder. "You won't regret this. People will talk of this for ages. You will become a living legend when you're done, just like ol' Tyven The Blade himself." With one final nod Jeret turned to leave.

As the Smile disappeared into the crowd, Kestus sat for a moment longer, turning the details over in his mind. Two nights. That gave him time to prepare, scout the High City, plan out every move.

Kestus slipped out of the tavern, the cold night air biting at his skin as he stepped into the labyrinth of the Undercity once more.

The streets were alive with muffled sounds: distant footsteps, hushed voices, the clanking of metal against stone. Something about the city felt different tonight, the feeling from the night before returned, as if the city was caught in someone's grip, strangling and unable to breathe.

Pulling his hood tighter, Kestus moved swiftly, his mind already spinning through the steps he'd need to take before the heist. The parchment Jeret had handed him was useful, sure, except Kestus trusted nothing that didn't come from his own eyes.

Secondhand information had a way of getting people killed.

He wouldn't waste a moment. Under the cover of darkness, he would travel to the High City and study every escape route, every blind spot, every guard rotation; knowledge was a power as ancient as any artifact.

- - - - - - - - - - - - - - - -

As he approached the boundary between the Undercity and the High City, the divide of Tare'Envel came into view. Swaying torchlight marked the edges of the wealthier district, casting long, shifting shadows over the crumbling buildings of the slums. Above, the spires of the High City pierced the night sky, their silhouettes a sharp reminder of who held control in this city.

Kestus paused in the darkness, his sharp gaze sweeping the scene. Guards patrolled in pairs, their boots crunching against the cobblestones. Their armor gleamed faintly in the light—a deliberate show of strength, a warning to anyone from the Undercity who might think of crossing over.

He took a deep breath, steadying himself. The boundary ahead was just another obstacle, like so many before it. His motions were quiet and intentional, as he melted into the shadows. Tonight wasn't about risk; it was about preparation, learning the rhythms of the enemy.

The burden of what lay ahead pressed down on him as he moved deeper into the night.

The Shiftscape Bracer wasn't just another job. It wasn't just a score. It was a gamble.

One that could change everything—or destroy him.

And in the pit of his stomach, Kestus couldn't shake the feeling that this time, there might be no coming back.

CHAPTER 4

Whispers in the Moonlight

The air was cool as the High City loomed before Kestus, its towers bathed in moonlight, casting long shadows over the Undercity below.

The opulence of the highborn, the wealth glimmering in every corner, stood in stark contrast to the grime he'd just left behind. Kestus slipped into the darkness at the city's outskirts, his eyes scanning the towering walls of King Alikhan's castle as he made his way through the High City.

Lanterns swayed in the breeze, their dim glow creating ripples of light on the cobblestones. Guards stood at their posts, their faces emotionless, weapons shimmering under the moon. The walls of the palace were adorned with the sigils of the King's reign—rose covered banners that stretched high above him live ravens, cold and unwelcoming, just like the King they represented.

Crouching behind a stack of crates, Kestus pulled the parchment Jeret had given him from his cloak. In the faint light of a nearby streetlamp, he studied the map.

Two entry points were marked: one through the drainage tunnels beneath the city, the other via the market district that was part of a merchant's shop that bordered the castle walls.

The merchant shop route was faster and more exposed, requiring him to make his way through the packed and bustling Ivory Row and potentially scale a precarious wall. The tunnels, though longer and winding, offered more cover and spat out into the castle grounds.

Kestus ran his fingers over the map, his brow furrowed. The job was already risky enough. Safer didn't mean safe, even so it would have to do.

He folded the map and slipped it back into his cloak when movement caught his eye. Crouching lower, Kestus spied two guards walking through a nearby alley. Their conversation was quiet yet, it carried urgency, their faces tense in the lantern light.

"The Hushed were spotted near the west gate," one of them muttered.

Kestus froze. The Hushed again. Those twisted specters of the Undercity seemed to haunt every corner of Tare'Envel lately, leaving a trail of unease wherever they appeared.

The second guard spat on the ground. "King Alikhan won't tolerate them this close to his palace." With another hack, the woman spat again. "Did you hear there's talk of a spy in the castle? Some lowborn rat trying to get cozy with the Undercity rabble, no doubt."

"No way is there a spy. The castle is locked up tighter than a mouse in a trap. No gang would be stupid enough to test the King." The other guard replied with a laugh.

The second guard laughed along. "I don't know. Tyven the Blade has been making a name for himself for a few years now. Maybe he will try something like Ironhand did."

"Its Ironfist, and that brute was an idiot. He got lucky all he lost was a hand. The Blade though, fancy name—but when Captain RosenThorn returns, she will make quick work of the Blade and his gang. Have you heard, they're saying the war is over…" The two continued to speak as they turned a corner. Their voices fading into the distance.

Letting out a slow, quiet exhale, Kestus straightened and stretched the tension from his back. He resumed his surveillance, noting the guards' movements and routines, double-checking potential entry points. If the drainage tunnel failed, he'd need an alternative. Every detail had to be perfect.

Mistakes weren't an option.

Hours passed as Kestus worked, the night stretching on, his breath visible in the frigid air. The moon dipped lower in the sky, its pale light beginning to fade into the deep blues of approaching dawn.

Movement at the edge of his vision caused Kestus to stiffen, his hand instinctively moving to the dagger at his waist.

A soft, honeyed voice broke the silence.

"Even shadows can be caught."

Kestus turned sharply, his eyes narrowing as a figure stepped out from behind a corner.

"Only when luring out the light," Kestus replied, lowering his hand, though his posture stayed wary.

"Hello, Kestus." The woman smiled and took a few steps closer.

His voice dropped to a measured tone. "Hello, Ellia." Sliding his hand behind him, Kestus' fingers began to tap. "What is RavenHood doing here? I thought you already did your part."

Ellia grinned, leaning casually against the wall, arms crossed. "Uncle Filko told me someone accepted Tyven's gambit." She tilted her head slightly, loose bangs falling across her face as her gaze moved toward the towering palace. "So, congratulations. You're officially the biggest fool in Tare'Envel. Not even Talons would have been crazy enough to take this one on."

A frown settled over Kestus' face.

"I mean it is pretty ballsy—even for you, Kestus 'Quickhand'." She added, her grin widening.

Kestus chewed his lip, trying not to smile back. "Is that a compliment?"

She shrugged, pushing away from the wall and taking a few quiet steps closer, her boots like midnight making no noise against the stone.

"Maybe. If you survive." Ellis's eyes scanned Kestus, looking him up and down. He wore his trusty grey cloak, tattered from years of use. His boots—worn to the sole.

Kestus, the Beggar Thief.

"You're insane for going after the bracer. You do realize that, right? No one in their right mind would actually believe this thing is anything more than a fancy piece of gear." Ellis's friendly demeanor changed to frustration.

Kestus narrowed his eyes. "If it's so crazy, why's RavenHood keeping tabs? Did Uncle Sharp-Eye send you to steal the bracer from me?"

Eyes rolling, Ellia tongued her cheek. "Who do you think gave Jeret the intel? Who do you think made the map in your pocket? I don't need *you*—to get this job done, Quickhand. I'm the Raven at your back, watching over you."

Kestus stared at her, expression neutral but his thoughts raced. "You're the spy in the castle?!"

Unable to help herself, Ellia laughed. "No. I am no spy. Yeah, I did most of the recon myself but only on the outside. We have someone else on the inside too. If you make it in, you'll meet her. She's the spy Tyven paid for. You fool, I am the Shadow's Wing. Spying is for thieves."

Her gaze shifted back to the castle, her voice lowering slightly. "Filko might be ambitious, but he's not an idiot. The King's palace is locked down tighter than it's ever been, Kestus. King Alikhan's been ramping up security for weeks. There's talk of secret shipments and strange visitors. Plus the sudden appearance of the bracer? No one knows where the King got it from or what it can actually do. If it's as powerful as the rumors say, you're stepping into a whole new level of danger. The King will want it back…"

Kestus kept his expression blank, though her words settled heavy in his chest. Hearing it all from Ellia

—the Shadow's Wing herself, she was Filko Sharp-Eye's niece—the heir of RavenHood, one of the greatest assassins in history. It made the stakes feel sharper, more tangible.

He studied her, and she returned his gaze, deep and assessing.

"So what's your angle, Ellia? Here to warn me off?" Kestus rubbed his thumb against his fingertips.

Her smirk returned, her eyes catching his tell. "Not really. Just wanted to see the madman for myself. Filko didn't think anyone would take this job. Thought the recon was easy money, but here you are, scouting the castle like it's another day in the Undercity. Gotta admit, I'm impressed. You're RavenHood material, Quickhand. I'd be happy to have you."

Glancing from the castle to the woman cloaked in black, Kestus said nothing. Ellia stood alert, yet relaxed—clearly confident in her skills and ready for anything. The feathers that adorned her cloak danced in the wind.

She stepped closer, her voice dropping to a near whisper. "I'll tell you this. If you pull this off, it's going to shake things up in ways you can't imagine. The gangs. The King... We're all watching. You're the spark, Kestus. Light the fire, and everything burns. You'll flip Tare'Envel upside down. And Alikhan the Stern? He won't let that go unanswered. His wrath will be something the gangs can't outrun. There'll be chaos. RavenHood will be ready. Will you? Will you accept the consequences of your actions?"

Their eyes locked, a silent understanding passing between them, thick with the weight of the city's undercurrents.

Then Ellia stepped back, pulling her hood up as the pale hints of dawn bled into the sky. The shadows folded around her as she faded into the remnants of night.

"Good luck, Quickhand," she called as she disappeared. "You'll need it."

Kestus stood still for a moment, her words echoing in his mind. A part of him knew she was right, even so, he couldn't turn back now. The prize was too great, the stakes too high.

Jeret and Tyven would track me down if I ran.

He finished his surveillance, noting the final details, before retreating into the Undercity and back to his home.

By the time dawn finally broke, he had made his way back to his safehouse. As he lay on his bed, staring at the ceiling, Ellia's visit still lingered in his thoughts.

This wasn't just another job.

"That's right!" Kestus sat up. "It isn't a normal job, so I need to make it one." Hurrying to his table, he began pulling out scraps of information about the castle, the Crimson Guard, the vault and all the theories on how to crack it.

"Two nights. In two nights, I need to figure out how to break into the most secure vault ever created. Easy."

CHAPTER 5

The Silent Approach

Two nights later, Kestus stood at the mouth of the drainage tunnel snaking beneath the castle grounds, his tattered cloak pulled tightly around him. The night air clung to him like a wet shroud, its chill biting into his bones. He barely noticed.

His focus was locked on the task ahead—retrieving the Shiftscape Bracer from King Alikhan the Stern's heavily fortified vault. This tunnel was his point of entry, a hidden artery connecting the underbelly of Tare'Envel to the opulent palace above.

The High City loomed over him, jagged rooftops stretching skyward like crooked fingers clawing at the stars. The damp earth and the scent of stale water hung heavy in the air.

Kestus felt the pressure of the city pressing down, as though the stones themselves were watching, waiting. One mistake, and the city would close its fingers around him, dragging him into its depths forever.

"Here we go," he muttered.

Nearby, Jeret waited with a small group of Starstriders, their job, to secure Kestus' exit route. Another group had already positioned themselves in the High City, just outside the castle. The group wore nothing to show their affiliation. They wouldn't enter the castle, however, their presence was a reminder of the stakes. Jeret, sharp as the daggers he carried, embodied Starstride's ruthless efficiency.

Kestus and Jeret had history, still that meant little in the Undercity. If the heist went south, Starstride wouldn't hesitate to cut their losses. Jeret had been upfront about that since the beginning.

"Starstride has your back in case anyone else tries to interfere," Jeret had said before they took their position. "Once you're inside the castle though, only that RavenHood spy can help. Quickhand, when you pull this off, you'll have earned a seat at the table. Porox's tongue, you could buy your own table!" With a stern look Jeret pulled out his best smile. "Good luck kid. We'll be waiting here for you."

A seat at the table wasn't what Kestus cared about.

The web of underworld politics was best navigated from the shadows, not at its center. Still, he preferred staying on the outskirts of it all. Right now, his only concern was the job. Next steps could wait—if he survived.

"Get in and get out," he whispered, stepping into the tunnel.

I got this.

- - - - - - - - - - - - - - -

The air inside was cold and dry, brushing against him like a ghost's moan. Moss and grime coated the slick walls, and the faint trickle of water echoed in the darkness. Each step was deliberate, his boots gliding soundlessly over the damp stone. As he ventured deeper, the passage narrowed, the walls seeming to press in on him.

The incline was grueling, seeming to span miles. The damp floor offered no traction. Kestus' breath came heavier with every step, his muscles burning from the climb. He resisted the urge to push faster; recklessness now would only sap his strength before the real challenge began

A distant light illuminated the end of the drain.

"Just a little further." He pushed on.

At last, the tunnel opened into a small service courtyard hidden from the main castle grounds.

Kestus pulled his hood tighter and crept toward the shadows, the force of the palace pressed down on him like a giant's hand.

Moonlight cast pale beams over ebony statues of forgotten Kings, their faces weathered and worn. The courtyard was surrounded by immaculate hedges, trimmed to geometric perfection. The serene beauty of the scene clashed with the tension coiling in Kestus' chest. Beyond those towering walls lay the treasure he was risking everything to claim.

A lone guard stood at the castle's entrance, idly pacing beneath a flickering lantern. His breath fogged and hung in the air. His posture was loose and unbothered—unaware of the predator stalking him from the depths of night.

Kestus studied the man's movements, counting the rhythm of his steps, the moments he turned his back, the slight sway in his stance that spoke of boredom.

Following the wall to its peak, Kestus lowered himself deeper into the shadows, as he watched an archer staring down into the courtyard. They were hard to make out, and Kestus wasn't positive if the guard was looking his way; due to the hood concealing their face. However, they hovered there for what seemed like hours, peering down in his direction.

Keep walking. Go on. Go on. Walk!

The archer noticed something and leaned off the edge to get a better look. When a heavy gust blew, lifting the end of Kestus' cloak to flap in the wind. With reflexes like lightning, Kestus snatched the loose fabric in an instant and pulled the cloth tightly to himself. Belly to the ground, he gazed up at the archer. Their hood was pulled back now and Kestus could clearly see their face looking down right at him.

Their gazes met and for a moment Kestus couldn't breathe. Piercing green eyes were focused on him and red lips twisted to reveal a mouth of gleaming teeth. Ellia had caught him. With a small wave, she pulled her hood up and resumed her patrol.

Not a spy...Feck. Quickhand, the Beggar Thief, caught by the Shadow's Wing. She will never forget this.

Eyes focused ahead once more, when the moment came, Kestus slipped forward like the wind—his dagger sliding free from his belt with practiced ease. The guard under the archway turned, his mouth opening to form a word that never came.

In a flash, Kestus closed the distance, one hand

clamping over the man's mouth while the other drove the hilt of his dagger into his temple. There was a quiet gasp, a faint exhalation, and then silence. The guard's body slumped into Kestus' waiting arms, heavy, yet manageable.

Hopefully she saw that.

With a grunt, Kestus dragged the unconscious man into the hedges, careful to tuck him deep into the dense greenery where he wouldn't be found.

Kestus worked quickly, stripping the guard of his gray and crimson uniform. The armor was well used and sturdy, the thick fabric cold to the touch as Kestus slipped into it, adjusting the leather straps until it fit snugly over his thin frame.

The disguise wasn't perfect—the fit was off, and the boots were large—but it would do.

Straightening, Kestus took a calming breath, draping his cloak over his shoulder like a cape and tucking his tools discreetly into the pockets of the uniform. The guard's helmet rested uncomfortably on his head, thankful that the visor would help conceal his face.

If you kept the visor down, I wouldn't have been able to sneak up on you so easily.

Now dressed as one of the palace's own, Kestus gave one more glance up at the wall to see if he still had an audience. With no trace of Ellia, he strode toward the entrance. His posture mimicked the indifferent gait of the castle guard he had been observing.

As he passed through the stone archway, the muted hum of the castle's nightly routine enveloped him.

Blending seamlessly into the flow of movement, Kestus walked with purpose behind a patrol of two guards. As long as things kept going smoothly, each step brought him closer to his goal.

CHAPTER 6

The Way to the Vault

The castle was a marvel of excess. Vaulted ceilings soared high above, chandeliers of crystal cast flickering candlelight across polished marble floors that seemed to stretch on forever. Gilded arches framed every corridor, their intricate designs reflecting the soft, golden glow.

Every inch of the castle screamed of wealth, power, and a complete disregard for the struggles of the city beneath it.

Kestus couldn't help but feel a sharp pang of resentment. This sumptuousness had been built on the backs of the Undercity—the same people the King had abandoned.

His boots echoed faintly on the marble as he paced through the halls, head bowed slightly as though lost in thought. In truth, his eyes darted to every shadow and corner, constantly scanning.

He unfolded a small parchment from beneath the guard's tunic. Ellia had done her part, securing this map of the castle's layout and ensuring his disguise could get him inside unnoticed.

Still, the map was far from perfect. Rooms were not where they were supposed to be, and corridors twisted in ways the parchment hadn't prepared him for.

"Where are the stairs? Nothing's right on this fecking thing." Kestus muttered under his breath, his irritation rising.

The vault lay deep beneath the palace, far from the glittering halls where nobles schemed and feasted. Said to be impenetrable, the vault was protected by more than just guards. Rumors of its defenses had sparked endless speculation, spawning legends that had only fueled Kestus' determination. Every vault had a weakness, and he had spent his past couple days unraveling this one.

If only he could find the damned stairs.

As he moved deeper into the maze-like castle, he quickened his pace as he grew frustrated. This place was similar to the Undercity, with its twisting corridors, but he didn't have years to master it

It's too quiet. Where are all the guards? This place should be packed with patrols.

Kestus rounded a corner and nearly collided with a young maid carrying a tray of linens. She stepped to the side and froze, her eyes widening as her grip faltered. For a split second, he thought she might drop the tray. She steadied it, and quickly bowed her head in apology.

Kestus' pulse raced as he forced himself to keep walking, his stride steady and more natural—retaking on the guards posture. He could feel her gaze on him, prickling like a knife in his back.

Desperate not to blow his cover, he strained his ears, listening for her footfalls retreating down the hall.

Nothing.

Please don't be there.

Glancing over his shoulder, he saw her still standing there, her expression not one of fear, more curious—puzzled, as though she were trying to place him.

Damnit. Why didn't you just keep walking?

Heart pounding, he decided to test his gamble. Quietly, so softly it was almost a breath, he muttered the passphrase Jeret had insisted he memorize.

"The wind carries the wings."

The maid's face changed instantly. Her lips twitched into the faintest smile, and she gave a nearly imperceptible nod.

Relief washed over Kestus. Keeping his composure, he didn't let just how nervous he truly was show. If this was the spy Ellia had promised, his gamble had paid off. If not, his entire plan was about to fall apart in an instant.

"And so, it carries the truth..." The girl peeked behind Kestus, looking down the hall, then inspected their surroundings before taking a step closer. "Did I say it right? I couldn't remember if it was 'carries' or 'brings' or 'holds.'"

Letting out a slow, steady sigh, Kestus nodded, walking closer to the girl. She was younger than he expected, her dark hair was pulled tight into a white bonnet, her green eyes were large and full of excitement.

Now Kestus knew why the interior map was so scattered—this girl wasn't even blood-sworn to RavenHood yet. This was her blood-rite.

Pretty risky allowing a novice to do this kind of spy work. What is Filko thinking? She could get someone killed. Could have gotten me killed!

With a furrow of her brow, her cheeks grew red as she spoke. "Cutting it close. I expected to run into you an hour ago. My shift is almost over, and you still need to swap your outfit."

"I need the way down." Kestus glanced around the two of them, urgency in his voice.

Still alone. Where are the guards? Why is it so quiet?

Her frown became a scowl. "No introduction or anything? Well, pleased to meet you, Thief." Her expression said otherwise. "Here are your clothes. Change quickly." The maid pushed her tray into Kestus' arms, then turned her back.

"Wh—ju—I..." With a sigh, Kestus glanced to his left at the door. "Why do I need to change?"

"How did you ever earn your name, with a question like that?" she muttered to herself, still loud enough for Kestus to take offense. "You're dressed as a patrolling guard. This is the uniform for the King's palace guard—the one's part of whatever is happening down there. Or did you want to get caught? Or have someone ask you a thousand questions and then get caught? Or see you trespassing, get caught, and then get killed?" The girl put the back of her hand to her forehead and let out a kind of squeal. "Hurry up already! We don't have all night!" With a stomp she began tapping her foot. "Talons would've known..."

"What was that?"

"I said hurry up!" The spy snapped.

Succumbing to the girl, Kestus undid the leather straps and dropped the guard's uniform to the floor, removing his tools from the pockets.

"Lose the torn blanket. No guard would be caught dead wearing that thing. The King would probably execute you if he caught you in that thing. Probably just for the crime against fashion," she ordered.

Holding his cloak, Kestus squeezed the fabric tight. She was right. The cloak was old, he had to let it go. It was thoughtless to have brought it. Leaving it here was necessary.

"Listen,Spy, be sure to get this back to me." Handing his cloak to the girl, Kestus finished putting on the new uniform. The color was pure white with gold inlaid in the cuffs and seams. The fabric was as light as silk and fit him better, allowing for quicker movement. The boots were pure black leather and his exact size.

Much better, but how do the guards keep this thing clean?

Trying to rub away a small smudge, Kestus caught the spy male a face close to disgust, as she picked up his cloak. "I'll be sure to save the ashes for you." She turned and started to walk away.

"Wait!" Kestus hissed as loud as he could without yelling. "Where are all the guards?"

"With everything going on, the King has the majority of guards patrolling closer to his chambers. I'm guessing he didn't want too many people around whatever is happening downstairs." Again the girl turned away when she finished.

That's good news at least. If I'm quick, I shouldn't see any more guards. That'll make getting out easier.

"Hey—you still haven't told me where the stairs are!" Arms crossed over his chest, Kestus could feel his fingers tapping his sides.

"Oh! Sorry... Go through that door," she pointed to the door to Kestus' right. "Behind the tapestry, you'll find the stairwell. That's what took me the most time, but I found it." Without turning back to look at the thief, the maid lifted her other hand to silence him. "Before you ask, 'What's down there?' I don't know. No one is allowed down there. Getting you that outfit was difficult enough. And I'm not hearing a 'thank you' or 'I know this must have been dangerous for you' or 'I'm so glad to have someone of your caliber to assist me with this mighty task.'"

Kestus blinked and held his tongue, silently taking in the information she was sharing.

"Anything else?" he asked, once she took a break from talking.

A sudden realization flashed across her face. "Oh

actually yes there is. I've noticed a lot of nobles going down there but no one's come out yet. Whatever it is, it seems... different. They're all dressed for something. The guards seem more on edge too. They say the King has been acting out of the ordinary; since his daughter's been out to war and he's been spending more time with his lurky advisor." Tapping a finger to her lip, the spy organized her thoughts. "Well that's it. Good luck, Thief. You really seem like you need it."

"Me?! You—" The girl had already turned the corner before Kestus could finish what he was saying.

I will let Ellia know exactly what I think of her "spy". Fecking kid.

Pushing through the door, Kestus took long, slow breaths to calm himself. He wasn't going to let his interaction throw off his mission.

Looking around the room and he was surprised at how lackluster it was. The room held a table and chairs atop a lavish handwoven rug, and that was all. There were no shelves or table settings; the room felt empty and without purpose. The tapestry hung on the opposite end of the room from where he stood. It matched the rug—lines of silver thread wrapped with blue, woven into the tassels.

Kestus slipped through, brushing the tapestry to the side, like the mouth of a snake, the staircase devoured him. Descending the hidden narrow spiral steps into the depths of the castle, he braces himself for what he might find.

As he proceeded deeper, the air grew thick. The light from the upper floors faded, replaced by a glow of mounted torches on the hallway below; with each step, the flame's shadows seemed to stretch up the stone wall behind him.

At the bottom of the staircase, he found himself in a long empty corridor. The walls were lined with intricate carvings—scenes of gods and monsters, their forms twisted in an eternal struggle. Among the carvings was one of Porox and Thylarn, locked in their great battle of sky and earth.

The Separation of Fate, where Porox divided the spirit from the physical. This would fetch a hefty price.

Then he caught sight of a strange vivid piece of art. A long, snake-like creature floating in a black abyss, its body adorned with long jointed arms and claw-like slashes across its scales. Its skull, resembling that of a lizard, was cracked open. Its chest, humanoid in shape, was exposed with decayed ribs, and the most grotesque detail of all—a mass of bone and flesh, some parasitic creature, feasted upon the creature's exposed brain.

"What the hell?" Kestus muttered under his breath, unsure of what he had just seen.

Just keep moving.

Hurrying through the corridor, he kept his head down, unwilling to be distracted any further from the other hanging depictions.

Eventually, he reached a fork in the path.

To the right, a faint, otherworldly glow seeped from beneath a set of massive double doors. Kestus could tell that whatever was happening behind those doors, the King and his nobles were likely there. The space between left him anxious, as if there was an unseen presence suffocating him.

To the left, a torch sat above a brick archway—unlit—leaving the end of the hall in darkness. The shadow beyond felt welcoming, eager to greet the thief. Behind this door, Kestus knew in his gut, lay the King's vault.

CHAPTER 7

The King's Vault

Examining the door for traps, Kestus used a torch from the main hallway to inspect every brick and crack. His sharp eyes searching for any sign of an alarm or hidden mechanism.

Strange. It looks clear? This is too easy.

With a deep breath, Kestus reached for the handle. His heart pounded in his chest, the tension in his fingers making the latch awkward to grip. Slowly, he pulled the heavy wooden door open.

"No traps. No alarm. No lock," he mumbled, his voice tinged with disbelief.

Standing at the threshold of the King's vault, heart hammering against his ribs despite the stillness in the air, the sight before him was nothing short of breathtaking. Torchlight spilled into the chamber, revealing a space that felt worlds apart from the dark and shadowed underbelly of Tare'Envel.

The floor gleamed with polished crystal. Veins of silver and gold ran through its surface, catching the light and giving the room an ethereal glow, as if the ground itself was spun from wealth. The stone felt and sounded like walking on metal rather than stone or glass. He could feel the cold through his boots and Kestus couldn't exactly tell, however, there was a weight to this place, as if each step he took was heavier here.

The walls bore paintings of the kingdom's past— battles won by previous Kings, treaties signed, and the coronation of King Alikhan. Towering pillars reached toward a ceiling painted with a vivid rendition of the night sky. Overhead, a massive chandelier sparkled, its crystal ornaments casting fractured beams of light across the room.

Kestus stood in awe. Unable to speak or think. This was a sight no one from the Undercity would even believe.

Who would ever want to hide this place?

At the far end of the chamber, nestled between two grand columns, stood the vault itself. Its imposing steel door contrasted sharply with the room's splendor—cold, harsh, and unyielding. This was not meant to inspire awe; it was meant to deter.

Kestus approached cautiously, his steady gaze

studying the structure. The vault door was locked.

Of course.

However, it lacked the magical protections told about in stories, it seemed King Alikhan relied on rumor and intimidation of the chamber itself to ward off intruders.

The faintest smirk touched Kestus' lips.

The King thought I'd be afraid of the magic of stories? He underestimated me.

Cracking his knuckles, he knelt before the door and got to work. Pulling tools from the pockets of his uniform, he inserted a pick into the lock. The mechanism was old but complex, a relic of master craftsmanship.

Beads of sweat started to form on his brows as he coaxed the tumblers into place, his practiced hands moving with precision.

This lock reminded him of the one he had cracked two years ago in the city of Reftan, during another job for Starstride. Jeret had wanted a rare ruby from a jeweler called the Solemn Stone. That vault had taken nearly two hours to open and cost him seven different picks.

That job almost went sideways when the jeweler happened to catch Kestus as he plucked the stone from the vault along with the grey silk fabric that Kestus wove into a cloak. In the end, he had escaped, in the nick of time, with the treasure and a nice little bounty. He hadn't been to Reftan since.

Lost in thought, Kestus nearly missed the satisfying click as the tumblers aligned.

He couldn't help but grin. Unsure of how much time had passed, Kestus did know he just unlocked the King's impenetrable vault and didn't break a single pick doing it.

Well done, Quickhand—the King's Bane.

The vault door creaked open, releasing a thick rush of air. The scent of ancient stone filled his lungs as he stepped inside.

The interior of the vault was sparse, almost disappointingly so. Shelves lined the walls, filled with crowns, jewels, and gilded scrolls—valuable treasures, certainly, yet none of them were what Kestus had come for. However, at the center of the room, resting atop a simple pedestal, was the object that screamed for his attention.

It wasn't the Shiftscape Bracer he sought.

It was a dagger.

And also something more than a dagger. It was different... Not long enough for a sword, yet too large for a knife. It was captivating and utterly unique. Truly, one-of-a-kind.

A strange tension hung in the air around the weapon, as if the room was trying to pry itself apart from the dagger's presence. The blade shimmered faintly, its edges unnaturally sharp, and the hilt adorned with silver. A strange emerald like gem was embedded in the dagger. Looking closer, a green cloud twisted inside like mist thrashing through a storm. Kestus could feel a faint hum emanating from the thing, like a heartbeat just out of sync with his own.

This wasn't just treasure. It was something dangerous.

What are you?

Kestus hesitated. Something about the dagger called—pulled at him. It wasn't what he had come for, and yet there was an importance to it, a mystery that made it seem as though the weapon held a secret begging to be discovered. His fingers brushed against the hilt, sending a jolt up his spine. For a brief moment, the substance within the emerald colored gem swirled faster, as if it were alive, responding to his touch.

"This isn't what I came for," he growled, his brow furrowing.

Suddenly aware, he noticed his breathing had become shallow and irregular. Yet, deep down, he knew leaving the dagger behind was not an option.

Beyond its sharp edge it possessed something—a strength, a power, a purpose.

Reluctantly, Kestus slid the ornate billhook dagger into his belt beside his meager looking one. Its mass felt right at his side, almost familiar, as though it belonged to him.

With one final glance around the room, he resumed his search for the true prize.

Damnit...*The bracer isn't here. I need to hurry out of here, but I can't leave empty handed. Feck.*

Carefully sealing the vault behind him, he retreated across the grand chamber and back into the main hallway. Every step, every motion, was deliberate as he erased any trace he may have left.

The dagger tapped lightly against his leg as he moved, a constant reminder of the risk he had taken. There would be no question that a thief had been present as soon as King Alikhan opened his vault,

The lack of security was the wrong choice for you. He won't know it was me. Well, as long as I'm a mile away from here when he checks.

Kestus started down the hallway, closing the door to the chamber behind him and returning his torch to its place on the wall. Just as he was about to head back upstairs, a sound stopped him.

It was faint at first, an indistinct noise coming from the opposite end of the hallway—the room he had ignored earlier. His curiosity flared, tugging at him with an unseen hand.

Unable to resist, Kestus crept closer. Each step brought him nearer to the heavy wooden doors, their surface marred with strange, unfamiliar carvings.

Pressing his ear against the wood, he hoped to make sense of the noise, but the thickness of the doors muffled what was happening on the other side. Green hues leaked through the thin cracks in the frame, pooling faintly on the floor like something supernatural, and alive.

Feck. I know I have to go in. Feeeck, I'm going to regret this.

With slow, steady hands, Kestus pushed the doors open just a crack and peered inside.

With a sudden gasp, his heart stopped.

CHAPTER 8

The Bloody Cathedral

The room beyond was unlike anything Kestus had ever seen—a vast underground cathedral, so immense it felt as though it stretched into the very bowels of the earth.

The chamber was surrounded by towering stone pillars, the heights of which disappeared into the suffocating darkness above, where no light dared reach. Ghostly shadows appeared to dance as strange vibrant shades of green torchlight flickered along the walls,

Inexplicably embedded within this underground room and deprived of sunlight, stained glass windows glowed in subdued hues. The grotesque images they formed depicted twisted figures in torment—souls writhing in never-ending agony. The focal point of the cathedral, an immense stained glass window, looming like a silent judge, demanding everyone's attention.

It depicted the banished goddess, drenched in blood.

The godess' hollow eyes seemed to follow Kestus, staring through him as if it knew his every thought. Its mouth was captured in an eternal scream —caught between ecstasy and agony—making it impossible to discern whether the deity reveled in the suffering or abhorred it.

The oppressive atmosphere pressed heavily on Kestus' chest, vibrating with a low, almost imperceptible hum that made his teeth ache. It was a space that demanded reverence, even from those unwilling to give it.

A wide stone staircase descended into the heart of the cathedral. At its base, a semi-circle of nobles had gathered. Their fine, silken robes shimmered faintly in the emerald glow, rippling as they swayed to the cadence of a low, rhythmic chant. The words they spoke were ancient and indecipherable, yet the intent behind them was unmistakably dark.

"Koreth dah sowe maiy Blu Vess!"

They repeated as one.

"Koreth dah sowe maiy Blu Vess!"

Standing at the center of the ritual, commanding all attention, was King Alikhan the Stern.

He was an authoritative and ominous figure who dominated the space. His ceremonial robes glimmered with golden embroidery that shown bright as the light, his eyes were riveted on the towering stained-glass godess above. The Shiftscape Bracer, the object of Kestus' yearning, warn on his wrist.

Its dark metal absorbed the torchlight around it, creating an aura that seemed to reject the very concept of illumination. Kestus' stomach tightened as he realized just how close he was to his goal. Yet, the sight of the bracer brought no sense of triumph, only unease.

Surrounding the nobles were the Hushed—silent, pale figures cloaked in flowing white robes, their faces obscured by thin ivory veils. Like statues carved from bone, they stood unnaturally still, radiating a sense of wrongness that seemed to distort the air.

Kestus had never been this close to them before. Their reputation as specters of death was terrifying enough, now seeing them in person made the stories feel inadequate.

Were they allies of King Alikhan? Or was the King merely a pawn in their enigmatic schemes? The scene unfolding before Kestus offered no answers, only more questions.

The King removed and raised the Shiftscape Bracer high above his head. The nobles' chanting grew louder, their voices rising in feverish intensity.

"Koreth Dah Sowe Maiy BLU VESS!"

The sound reverberated through the cathedral, shaking the stone walls and filling the atmosphere with an unbearable tension. Every syllable dripped with an unspoken promise—of power, of ruin, of something far greater than the mortals chanting in this sacred, accursed space.

Kestus gripped the edge of the doorway, his knuckles white as he forced himself to stay still. His instincts screamed at him to run, to escape this place and whatever terrible ritual was taking shape.

Except he couldn't leave—not without the Shiftscape Bracer.

He had come too far to turn back now.

"My fellow brethren of Sangretis, bask in her aura!" King Alikhan's voice boomed, captivating everyone in the room. "We stand here today not as worshippers of our lost god, but as beacons! Tonight, we will light the torch to bring her back to us! To ME!"

In a slow, deliberate motion, King Alikhan handed the bracer to a cloaked servant who stepped forward reverently. The two exchanged hushed words too quiet for Kestus to hear.

The servant, head bowed low, cradled the bracer in his hands as though it were a child. With careful steps, he brought it into a small chamber off of the cathedral's main hall.

Kestus' instincts flared to life.

This was the moment. His moment.

He quickly scanned the room. The upper level of the cathedral was framed by a balcony that would allow him to slip across unnoticed. If he could reach the small chamber before anyone else entered, he'd have the bracer in his hands before the King or the Hushed even realized he was there.

This can work!

Inhaling deeply, Kestus closed his eyes as he focused inward, centering himself. Then, he moved into action. Slowly, carefully, he crept across a wooden beam that stretched above the main floor. Once above the chamber door, he crouched against a support beam, concealing himself in the shadows.

Looking down, he saw no easy way to descend without drawing attention. The only option was to use his Shadow Step.

Quickhand. A name he had earned from countless heists, however, no one knew the secret behind his speed. It was a secret he guarded fiercely, one he barely understood himself. Shadow Step, it wasn't magic in the traditional sense, nor was it quite stepping at all. To Kestus, it was more like slipping between the cracks of the world—an instantaneous movement to any point he could see. A teleportation of sorts, silent and without fanfare.

It was his greatest weapon, except it came at a cost. Every use drained him, leaving him lightheaded and weak. He saved it for moments like this—when there was no other way.

In a single, fluid motion, Kestus activated the ability.

The world around him shifted, collapsing the distance between his perch and the chamber's entrance in an instant.

One moment, he stood on the edge of the cathedral's frame. The next, he perched silently just outside the chamber door, his presence unnoticed. To any onlooker, it would seem as though he had fallen from the balcony and landed perfectly on the ground, in the blink of an eye.

Wasting no time, Kestus slipped into the small chamber, his movements fluid and soundless. The servant had just placed the bracer on a stone pedestal and was murmuring words of reverence under his breath, too absorbed to notice Kestus lurking behind him.

The thief pressed himself into a shadowed corner, watching as the servant finished his whispered prayer. Without a second glance at the artifact, the servant turned and left, his footsteps fading as he returned to the main hall.

Lightheaded from his Shadow Step, Kestus exhaled slowly, releasing the breath he hadn't realized he was holding. Closing his eyes briefly, he tapped his index and middle fingers against his knees, counting to four before opening them again.

He was alone with the treasure, his prize, the Shiftscape Bracer.

Heart racing, not from fear, not from doubt, but from anticipation, he was finally standing before the legendary artifact. Deceptively simple, the Shiftscape Bracer sat atop the grey stone pedestal. The supernatural charm he had observed had vanished from its dark metal and now it appeared mundane and unremarkable, as if it were just a piece of equipment.

However, Kestus was no fool.

This was no ordinary object, he could feel it—the same faint pull he'd felt with the dagger. His eyes locked on the crystal gem embedded in the bracer. Unlike the dagger's swirling gem, this one was empty, hollow, as though waiting for something.

What are you waiting for?

Kestus didn't know if he was asking himself the question or the bracer.

Fingers brushing the cool surface of the metal, he felt a sudden shock of strength—a surge of power — run through his body as his flesh touched the surface of the bracer. The energy was raw, untamed, alive—a tempest coursing through his veins. It felt as though the bracer itself had a will, a consciousness, that was now aware of him.

The power flooded through Kestus, overwhelming and alien, he clenched his teeth. It was as if the artifact had chosen him, as if it had found something inside of him.

Remaining firm despite the noxious sensation that was creeping up his spine, he couldn't back down now.

He had done it.

The bracer was his.

At long last he held salvation, prestige, power... Then, a sudden scream tore through the cathedral, sharp and shrill, shattering the oppressive stillness.

Kestus' head snapped toward the sound. Wearily he hurried to the doorway to look out at the mania.

Beyond the chamber, in the main hall, King Alikhan

stood beneath the stained glass. His body trembled violently, his white ceremonial robes now soaked in crimson. The King looked like the depiction of the godess above him. Blood poured freely from a gash in his side—a wound that looked self-inflicted.

The chanting collapsed into chaos as the nobles began to scatter, their voices replaced with panicked cries.

The Hushed, eerily calm, moved with precision. Their ghostly forms gliding through the chaos, swords gleaming in the green torchlight. They let no one escape, closing in like predators herding their prey.

Not waiting to see what would happen next, with the Shiftscape Bracer in hand, Kestus activated his Shadow Step.

The world blurred, folding in on itself, and in a blink, he reappeared at the top of the stairs across the room.

Without hesitation, he bolted from the cathedral, yanking the enormous doors open and sprinting toward the spiral staircase. Behind him, the screams of the nobles echoed, mixing with the guttural, maddened laughter of King Alikhan.

Whatever dark ritual the King had unleashed, it was far beyond Kestus' understanding—and getting farther behind him, with each step he took.

"Run, run, run!" he urged, his breath ragged, his legs pumping harder.

Just run!

CHAPTER 9

The Weight of Power

Stumbling up the stairs, nearly tripping over himself in his desperation to escape the horrors below, Kestus' breath came in rapid gasps. Adrenaline coursing through his veins—urging him forward—he pushed past the tapestry concealing the passage. It flapped uselessly behind him as he carelessly knocked over a few chairs, sending them clattering to the floor. He didn't care. His thoughts were singular now.

Need to go. Have to get out.

He slammed into the stone wall of the hallway, pausing for just a second as his chest heaved. His mind raced, trying to recall the exact route he'd taken to get into the castle. The map he had memorized now felt like a blur in the fog of fear clouding his mind. He needed to get back to the drainage tunnel. If he could reach it, he'd be safe—

at least, as safe as he could be.

Heartbeat slowing slightly, another thought crept into his mind, Ellia and the castle spy.

Did they make it out?

The spy, while frustrating, had been his ally tonight. She had helped guide him when he was lost.

She had said she was waiting for me and that her shift was over. She must've gotten out. I hope she got out... That still leaves Ellia, though."

"Halt!" A deep commanding voice ordered from behind Kestus.

Pushing the thought to the back of his mind Kestus moved. Without a glance, he resumed his frantic sprint down the hallway. The sound of clanking metal, scraped along behind him.

"Stop there! Intruder! Intruder!" A second guard yelled, his boots picking up speed.

I have to lose them!

With the bracer in hand, the ornate dagger at his belt, and—at least for now—his head on his shoulders, Kestus knew the only way out would be to Shadow Step again.

Feeling his legs weaken and hearing the two guards behind him quicken, he knew there was no other way.

With a grimace, Kestus turned down a long stretch of hallway and activated his Shadow Step. The hallway folded before him, and with a single step he strode across the entire distance.

Barreling through the first door he saw, Kestus burst into the courtyard. The cold night air hit him like a slap, pointed and bracing. The statues that had seemed so ordinary earlier now loomed over him, larger than they ever were in life. Their stone gazes bore into him, judgmental and oppressive. The once—beautiful courtyard morphed into a maze of impending doom, every shadow a potential threat.

His eyes darted to the spot where he had knocked out the guard earlier. The body was gone. Kestus froze, his pulse thundering in his ears.

Did he wake up or did someone discover him? It doesn't matter. Feck, just keep going!

The crunch of a leaf under his boot snapped him out of his panic—everything was still. The hedges swayed gently in the breeze, and the courtyard lay quiet. He breathed a quiet sigh and pressed on, darting across the open space. The soles of his boots barely made a sound against the cobblestone path.

She's not stupid enough to go in after me. She flew

away hours ago. If she's still up there watching like a raven, Ellia will be running too. Everyone got out. Just keep going. Everyone got out.

Reaching the courtyard's edge, Kestus risked a glance back. Nothing but darkness and the cold whisper of the wind. The wall was empty of all its guards.

She got out.

So far his luck had held. At any moment, the castle could erupt into chaos. Guards could flood the corridors and the courtyard, cutting off any route of escape. He couldn't stay and watch, he had to keep going.

Ahead, the drainage tunnel came into sight. His way in was also his way out. The secret route, he eagerly slipped back inside, letting the cool dry air swallow him whole.

The tunnel was narrow, its air thick with the earthy scent of moss. Moisture dripped from the curved stone walls, slick beneath his fingertips as he steadied himself. His footsteps echoed softly in the gloom, still he welcomed the solitude. Here, at least, no one could reach him.

For now, he was safe.

He slowed his pace and let out a heavy breath, his head fell forward, exhaustion weighing on him, not just in his limbs but also deep in his chest.

Things had changed.

He couldn't shake the image of king Alikhan beneath the banished godess, his laughter rising above the screams of his dying nobles. The madness in the cathedral had been only the beginning; Kestus could feel it in his bones.

Tare'Envel was teetering on the edge of a nightmare, and Kestus—whether he liked it or not—was now at the center of it all.

CHAPTER 10

The Drainage Tunnel

As Kestus ventured deeper into the tunnel, the memories of the cathedral coiled around him, tightening their grip with every step. The images burned in his mind—King Alikhan's blood-soaked robes clinging to his body like a second skin, the nobles' terrified screams as their ritual unraveled into madness, and the bone-chilling silence of the Hushed, their ghostly forms moving with swords in hand.

And then, there was the godess.

The blood-drenched figure from the stained glass, its hollow, tormented eyes seemed to peer into his soul, judging him for what he had witnessed. No matter how far he ran, those eyes followed. Kestus had seen the Bloodied Vessel in all her splendor and it horrified him.

The chanting, the slaughter, and King Alikhan's laughter echoed endlessly in his mind. Even here, in the cold, damp tunnel, the burden of the cathedral's horrors bore down on him like a crushing tide. His grip tightened on the Shiftscape Bracer now secured around his wrist, its metal a small comfort against the relentless tide of memories.

The bracer pulsed faintly, emitting a subtle hum that vibrated through his skin and into his bones. It reminded him of the moment he first touched it —the raw, untamed power that had surged through him like wildfire. Now, with the immediate danger behind him, the full weight of that power settled heavily on his shoulders.

He couldn't deny it anymore. The bracer wasn't just an artifact; it was alive.

"I can't just give this away," he muttered, his voice barely audible against the quiet drip of the tunnel.

The words felt heavier than he intended, like an oath binding him to something he didn't yet understand. He couldn't let the bracer fall into the wrong hands—not after what he just saw.

But what is the alternative?

He didn't know how to control this power, and carrying it felt like walking on a knife's edge, one misstep away from disaster.

The tunnel stretched on, its damp, moss covered walls, slick beneath his fingertips. The air grew thicker with the stench of rot, as the rhythmic drip of water amplified the oppressive emptiness. Nevertheless, Kestus moved forward, every muscle in his body burning, tense, tired, but alert.

"Just a bit further," he whispered, his voice a subtle reassurance to himself.

Rest was a distant dream. His thoughts raced too much for him to relax, consumed by what lay ahead, and what he had left behind.

The tunnel ended ahead, and a faint flicker of light caught his eye. He stopped, his breath catching in his throat.

Torchlight.

His heart slammed in his chest as he crouched low. Watching the faint glow dance against the tunnel walls, Jeret and the Starstride crew were supposed to meet him at the exit, except they wouldn't have been foolish enough to bring torches. Jeret knew better than to attract attention in a city like Tare'Envel, especially with the importance of the relic.

Something was wrong.

Kestus' instincts flared to life, a familiar chill crawling up his spine. He crept forward, sticking to the shadows, his movements planned and soundless. As he approached the light, his mind raced through possibilities—rival gang members, castle guards, or worse, the Hushed.

Whatever it was, Kestus knew one thing: the night wasn't done with him yet.

Dropping into a crouch, Kestus pressed himself against the cold, damp stone wall. His breathing came slow and soft, his heartbeat gradually falling back into rhythm. The shadows wrapped around him like a cloak as he inched forward, silent as the breeze that swept through the tunnel. His keen eyes strained against the dim light, focusing on the quivering glow ahead.

Just outside the tunnel's mouth, five figures stood silhouetted against the cool night air. The torchlight painted their jagged forms in a sinister orange glow. Kestus' stomach twisted.

Knife Point!

Their leader stood front and center—a scarred brute of a man with shoulders like a battering ram and a nose that had clearly been broken, reset, and broken again. His face was a cruel mask of hate and disdain, scrunched up to show how unhappy he was at everything around him. His lips twisted in a sneer as he idly flipped a dagger in his hand. The blade caught the torchlight with every rotation, gleaming like a predator's tooth.

"Feck." Kestus hissed under his breath, his pulse quickening.

Knife Point, they were the most brutal gang in Tare'Envel. Where Starstride favored cunning and leverage, Knife Point thrived on bloodshed and cruelty. If they were here, it wasn't a coincidence.

Either Starstride had set him up, or Jeret had been overwhelmed and left for dead. Neither possibility boded well.

Chest tightening, his mind trying to piece together the grim picture. Knife Point wouldn't move without a payday big enough to justify it, and that meant someone had offered them a hefty sum to intercept him and take the Shiftscape Bracer. His fingers brushed the artifact, and he felt it hum faintly, almost as if it were responding to the threat. Its weight seemed to double, a physical reminder of how high the stakes had become.

He suppressed a shudder and focused on the group. The Knife Point leader barked a gruff order, and two of his thugs began pacing the tunnel entrance, their torches casting dancing shadows that resembled hunting spears. The remaining three lingered close, their laughter thunderous and wrong, high pitched like coyotes.

Kestus melted deeper into the shadows, his mind

racing. Five against one was suicide. His Shadow Step would give him an advantage, except he had already used it three times tonight and he could already feel the fatigue in his muscles. If they caught his trail, they'd chase him across the city- and with the bracer in hand, every gang in the Undercity would eventually join the hunt.

Still as stone, Kestus waited, his breathing slow and steady. Creeping slightly closer, he studied their movements, their placement, and their leader's sharp gaze. The gang wasn't here to talk. They were here to kill and steal.

His jaw tightened. Whatever the next move was, he'd need to make it fast.

For now, he remained hidden, a shadow among shadows, listening to the Knife Point thugs as they laughed and taunted the darkness.

His head cleared as he began to make a plan. There would be no easy way out of this.

CHAPTER 11

At Knife's Point

Kestus pressed himself against the damp grime covered wall, further dirtying his castle guard uniform.

He had faced bad odds before, yet five armed thugs —especially when he already felt like he had been tossed off the roof of the castle—made him rethink his chances. He needed every advantage he could muster.

Scooping up mud, dirt, and water, he smeared the mixture deep into the white fabric, doing his best to darken the bright uniform.

I only have one chance at this.

Satisfied with his makeshift camouflage, he turned his focus to the next step.

Time for the distraction.

Kestus knelt, his eyes never leaving the group of thugs, his fingers searching the tunnel floor for something. Moving through thick cold water, they soon found a loose stone, smooth and chill to his touch.

"Soar with Trylarn's grace, If you do, i might just make it out of here alive," he whispered to the stone, offering it a prayer.

With a flick of his wrist, he sent the stone skittering across the ground. It went even further than expected and clattered loudly against the far wall, the noise echoing all the way to the tunnel and drawing the thugs' attention away.

"What was that?" one of them muttered, stepping toward the noise. The torchlight glinted off his ears, where the tips of small daggers hung like grim ornaments.

"Check it out and make it quick, Razortip," the leader growled. He didn't move from his spot, he just seemed to grow angrier, nostrils flaring as he frowned. The man's battered nose gave him the air of someone familiar with violence.

Two other thugs followed Razortip, their weapons held at the ready. Judging by their appearance, Kestus guessed they had similar nicknames. The brute on the left, with his flattened features, was probably *Clubface*, while the one on the right, gripping a blade in each fist, seemed like a good candidate for *Knuckleknife*.

This wouldn't be easy. *Broken Nose*, he named the leader, hadn't budged an inch, and waiting too long for the perfect moment could cost him dearly.

When the three men were just far enough from the others, Kestus tightened his grip on his trusty dagger.

Simple and reliable. We got this.

Moving like a striking viper, he darted from the drainage tunnel, his free hand lashing out to pierce a nerve cluster on the first thug's neck.

The man's eyes widened in shock and recognition just before he crumpled silently to the ground. Kestus didn't waste a second. Pivoting on his heel, he shifted his attention to the next target.

Move, move, move.

Broken Nose had only started to react when Kestus swung his dagger in a swift arc, the hilt smashing into the gang leader's already mangled nose. Blood sprayed, and Broken Nose's eyes went wide as they rolled to the back of his head as he fell hard to the ground, collapsing with a wet gurgle.

The crack of bone and the thud of the massive body hit the air simultaneously. The remaining thugs spun toward the noise, their eyes alert with alarm.

"Feck," Kestus muttered under his breath, frowning.

Didn't mean to do that.

"Get him!" Razortip snarled, charging forward with a guttural bellow, his dagger earrings flashing as they swung with each stride.

Kestus crouched, bracing himself as his heart pounded in his ears. The Shiftscape Bracer pulsed against his wrist, sending sharp jolts through his arm, urging him to use its power. The temptation was undeniable. His breathing quickened, the artifact's pull clouding his thoughts, it wanted to be unleashed. Yet, Kestus hesitated—he still didn't fully understand its power. Shadow Stepping was an option, however, exhaustion threatened to leave him delirious and vulnerable if he risked it now.

Razortip was on him in a flash, his dagger slicing through the air in a wild arc. Kestus barely ducked in time, the blade skimming his shoulder and leaving a shallow cut. Pain shot through him, sharp and immediate. The stolen guard uniform, designed more for appearance than function, offered no real protection. Gritting his teeth, Kestus rolled to his feet and drove his elbow into Razortip's abdomen. The thug grunted, staggering backward but he refused to fall.

Before Kestus could regroup, Knuckleknife lunged,

his twin blades aimed for Kestus' chest. Anticipating the attack, Kestus sidestepped, catching the man's wrist in a firm grip. With a hard twist, he forced the thug to drop one of his blades. Knuckleknife cried out in pain, doubling over as Kestus' knee struck his ribs with brutal force, sending him to the ground gasping for air.

Razortip roared in frustration, charging again with reckless fury. This time, Kestus was ready. Waiting until the last possible moment, Kestus slipped past Razortip—getting close—he grabbed the back of the thug's skull and used Razortip's own momentum to slam him headfirst into the tunnel wall. The thug crumpled to the ground in a heap, groaning.

Before Kestus could catch his breath, Clubface flanked him, closing the gap with surprising speed. Wielding a club in each hand, he swung with precision. Kestus ducked the first swipe and narrowly parried the second with his dagger, splinters flew as metal met wood.

"Puhhhf!" Kestus gasped, as one of Clubface's strikes landed cleanly against his ribs. The air rushed from his lungs, leaving him doubled over in pain. His fingers loosened, sending his trusty dagger flying off in a random direction. Agony radiated through his side, and he was certain at least one rib had fractured.

"How's that, Quickhand? Not as fast as they say, are

you?" Clubface sneered, using one of his clubs to lift Kestus' chin, forcing him to meet his gaze. Kestus winced and noticed Clubface's eyes looking down at his arm. "Looks like I'll be breaking that fancy little bracer off your wrist." Clubface jabbed Kestus in his ribs with his second club. "And believe me, I'll enjoy it more than you will. After what I do to you they'll call me, *the Bonecrusher!*"

With a triumphant yell, Clubface raised both weapons high, preparing to bring them down and shatter Kestus into pieces.

Watching the two clubs plummeting toward him, Kestus let out a guttural roar of his own, and activated his Shadow Step—unknowingly triggering the Shiftscape Bracer.

The artifact flared to life. Its glow engulfing him in a sudden burst of power.

The world dimmed beyond the darkness of night, plunging Kestus into a distorted void. The shadows around him writhed, alive with a strange pulse, as if the darkness itself was breathing. Clubface remained frozen, mid-swing, his face contorted in a silent battle cry. Torchlight hung onto his clubs, the flames trapped in a continuous crackle, forever breaking.

Kestus' footsteps made no sound in this strange realm. His surroundings felt unreal—muted, stretched, and warped. The cold stone beneath him had lost its bite, replaced by an unsettling numbness. Even the dripping water from the tunnel ceiling hung motionless, glimmering like suspended glass.

Each step was a battle. The air felt heavier than stone, clinging to him like an invisible weight. Yet, for all its suffocating resistance, the power thrumming through him urged Kestus onward. The Shiftscape Bracer pulsed on his wrist, its energy a burning ache that spread through his arm and into his chest.

He moved with purpose, circling Clubface, whose every detail stood out with unnatural clarity. The bulging veins on the thug's neck, the faint scar along his jaw, the dirt caked beneath his fingernails —everything seemed magnified in this never ending moment.

Kestus felt his heart hammering in his chest, the sound deafening in the silence. He felt the bracer tightening, its grip unrelenting, urging him to act, to strike.

Reaching Clubface's back, Kestus paused. The thug's muscles were locked mid-motion, the clubs raised high and ready to crush. Time itself seemed caged. Kestus shifted, steadying himself, and positioned himself ready to attack.

Energy burned like fuel. Exhaustion began to out way the bracer's influence. Kestus knew he had to end this.

Releasing his Shadow Step felt like snapping a thread.

The world lurched back into motion, the sudden rush of sound and movement disorienting him. Clubface, propelled by momentum, smashed his clubs into the dirt where Kestus had been standing. The impact reverberated through the thug's arms. He howled in pain, dropping both weapons. Tears fell like rain down Clubface's cheeks.

Before the man could recover, Kestus delivered a brutal kick to the man's spine, sending him sprawling face-first into the muck.

You can't keep this up, You need to make sure he doesn't get back up.

Kestus groaned, his voice low and ragged. He stood there, panting, his body screaming in protest. He wiped blood from his split lip, wincing at the sting of fresh cuts and bruises. Every breath sent waves of excruciating pain through his ribs.

"H-how did you do it?" Sobs puffed out of the man as he tried to crawl away with broken wrists. "It's not possible...you were there on the g-ground. On the ground!"

With a wince, Kestus kneeled down—picking up one of the man's splintered clubs.

He would've killed me if I didn't move. The impact nearly shattered his own clubs...

Raising the weapon high, the thug didn't even turn as the whistle of the wind sang, a brief sharp prelude, just before the *crack*! The club broke against the back of Clubface's skull.

Taking a moment to slow his racing heart, Kestus surveyed his surroundings.The Knife Point thugs lay scattered around him, battered and motionless. The fight had been closer than he cared to admit but he stood there, triumphant against the odds.

He knew his Shadow Step drained him, however, whatever had just happened felt worse. The Shiftscape Bracer pushed his body to new limits, dragging power from him in ways he couldn't fully grasp. And yet, for those brief moments, the strength it gave him had been undeniable, he had the power of a gos.

Footsteps echoed in the distance—more guards, or perhaps another group of thugs. Whoever they were, they were closing in fast.

With one last glance at the fallen Knife Points, Kestus ran. His movements were no longer careful, just swift, as he fled into the night.

CHAPTER 12

A Meeting in the Dark

The frigid air covered the city with a thin layer of moisture, the cold stung Kestus' bones as he navigated the Undercity of Tare'Envel. His clothes were damp and clung to his skin, amplifying the ache in his bruised ribs. Leaning briefly against the rough stone wall of an old bakery, he took a ragged breath. Every movement felt like a gamble against the pain threatening to steal his focus. Behind him, faint echoes of distant activity resounded through the narrow passageway, a reminder that the city's dangers never slept.

His fingers absently tapped against the Shiftscape Bracer on his wrist, its weight both a comfort and a curse. The artifact's power simmered beneath its metallic surface, humming faintly as if alive. Kestus couldn't help but shudder at the memory of King Alikhan holding the bracer beneath the unnatural glow of the cathedral's stained-glass windows. The ritual, the blood-soaked altar, the sinister intent—it all felt like an intricate puzzle he wasn't equipped to solve.

Several questions gnawed at him, each one more unsettling than the last. Could the King wield the same power now coursing through him? How was the artifact connected to that nightmarish ritual? And, most pressing of all, what did Tyven truly want with the Shiftscape Bracer? The thought sent a chill through Kestus, he did his best to push it aside. There would be time to piece it all together later—assuming he made it through the night.

Knife Point could still be after me. I need to keep moving.

Forcing himself upright, Kestus pressed on, delving deeper into the tangled mess of Tare'Envel's Undercity. The maze of narrow alleyways and crumbling stone facades felt like a world apart from the gleaming towers above. Shadows clung to every surface, and the faint crescent moonlight offered little relief. The air was thick with the stench of mildew, rotting wood, and the faint metallic tang of rusted iron, each corner an assault on the senses.

Moving swiftly, Kestus kept his head low and his ears open. He cursed under his breath, wishing he still had his cloak. Without it, he felt exposed, his face vulnerable to the gaze of anyone lurking in the gloom.

"I need something more. Next sheet I see, I'll steal. That'll be better than nothing and will at least get rid of this chill," he muttered, trying to rub some warmth into his hands.

A sudden clatter of footsteps from a nearby alley made him freeze. Flattening himself against the wall, Kestus strained his ears. He waited as the noise faded into the distance. It was enough to push him forward at a faster pace. Every stride became harder than the last, his body protesting against the tension of the night's events. Still, he pressed on, his mind fixed on the rendezvous point.

He would find Jeret—or answers.

Blending into the darkness, his footfalls were soft on the worn cobblestones. Every shadow seemed alive, shifting and twisting at the edges of his vision. Every faint noise—an echo of distant voices, the scrape of metal, or the rustle of a rat—carried the possibility of unseen danger. The Undercity was alive with menace, however, the steady pulsing energy of the Shiftscape Bracer on his wrist grounded him, soothing him in ways he was reluctant to admit.

Kestus navigated the twisting streets with practiced ease, each turn bringing him closer to his destination. Above the crooked rooftops, the jagged silhouette of an old church rose against the faint glow of the moon, a silent marker of his path. Wooden signs creaked overhead in the passing wind, their faded paint long since worn away by time. Rats darted through piles of debris, their sudden movements stirring the oppressive stillness of the Undercity.

He glanced over his shoulder, scanning for any sign of pursuit. Nothing. For now, at least, he was alone.

Turning down a narrow passage, Kestus slipped into an alley where the stone walls pressed close on either side, their surfaces slick with moss. A rusted lantern hung from a crooked post, its feeble flame casting long, restless shadow across the uneven road. The air here was thicker, heavy with the mingling miasma of decay and smoke.

Ahead, the alley opened into a small courtyard, its uneven stones slick with moisture. A broken fountain sat in the center, its basin empty and cracked. Beyond the fountain lay the entrance to a safehouse he and Jeret had used before— a forgotten alcove that had remained untouched amidst the chaos of the Undercity.

As Kestus moved closer, a distant movement caught his attention at the far end of the alley. His heart quickened, and he instinctively pressed himself against the wall, his form vanishing into the shadows.

A group of figures passed through the narrow lane, their voices low and unhurried, their laughter echoing faintly. They carried no torches, their shapes indistinct in the dark night. They moved with the careless confidence of people with nothing to fear.

Remaining motionless, Kestus' breathing was slow and controlled. He waited until the voices faded into silence, the figures disappearing into the distant streets.

"Easy, Quickhand. Not everyone is out to get you," he murmured to himself, though the tension in his body lingered.

I am almost there.

At last, his gaze settled on the faint outline of a figure near an archway just beyond the courtyard. The figure shifted slightly, and even in the dim light, the silhouette was unmistakable.

"Jeret," Kestus whispered, releasing some of the tension in his shoulders with a heavy sigh. .

Pushing off the wall, he stepped cautiously out of the darkness and moved toward the hidden alcove. His approach was swift, his movements as silent as the night around him. The faint glow of the lantern guttered behind him, casting a giant of a shadow ahead of him, as he closed the distance to where

Jeret waited.

CHAPTER 13

Safehouse

Jeret's face was pale, his features tense and drawn as Kestus approached. The night cast sharp lines across his expression. His legs were bouncing, hands trembling, he had dry lips—clearly from licking them too often, eyes darting back and forth. He did not look like a veteran of the streets at all.

That makes two of us.

When their eyes met there was a brief moment of relief for both of them.

"I was starting to wonder if you'd made it out," Jeret smiled, his lips barely moving. Glancing left and right, he gave a subtle nod toward the courtyard and began leading Kestus away from the rendezvous point. "I've been here a while. I'm feeling antsy, too many eyes have seen me. Almost pulled a knife on a scrapping tree branch. I've got a shack close by—hidden. No one knows about it."

Kestus clenched his teeth as a sharp pain shot through his ribs. Forcing himself to take a steadying breath, he pushed through the ache and fell into step beside Jeret.

Eyeing him, Jeret flashed one of his trademark grins.

"What a fecking night," he muttered as they moved deeper into the courtyard.

The scene around them was a direct contradiction to the High City. The air here was laden with decay, saturated by the unrelenting damp that seeped into everything. Walls that might once have been part of grand structures now sagged under the burden of neglect, their surfaces darkened with grime. Wild vines snaked through cracks, consuming what little remained intact

Puddles pooled in the uneven cobblestones, catching the faint light of rusted lanterns swaying on crooked posts. Broken crates and discarded belongings littered the ground, creating obstacles for anyone who dared to tread this forgotten corner of Tare'Envel. The stench of sewage hung heavy in the air, making it difficult to draw a full breath. Rats darted between shadows, their movements a constant reminder of the rot festering beneath the city's grandeur.

Kestus shrugged in an attempt to loosen the tension in his shoulders. His voice carried a sharp edge. "Ran into a bit of trouble. Right where you said you'd be waiting for me." He let the accusation hang between them.

Jeret took a deep breath and glanced around, his brow furrowed. "Trouble huh? Let me guess…more Knife Point?"

Kestus nodded grimly. Then he noticed Jeret was walking stiffer than usual, keeping his left arm slack and straight to his side. "Knife Point tried to grab the bracer from me as soon as I got out of the castle. I took out a grip of them. It wasn't easy though. One of them got me pretty good"

"They got us too. Some big bastard with a broken nose and his goons. We gave a few of them a bashing, but there were ten of them and only four of us. The boys and I got out, just not before some prick broke me arm with his clubs." Jeret cursed under his breath. "This complicates things. We both knew this job was hot. Still, with Knife Point involved it's going to be harder getting to Tyven. They'll be watching the Seventh Star, waiting for us."

"I dealt with my followers." Kestus' voice was strained, from both the pain in his chest and from the stench around them. "What matters now is getting out of the city for a bit. Need to lay low."

Jeret didn't argue.

The two continued walking until they got to a little shack. It wasn't much even in a city where all of the Undercity could be described as, "nothing much." The hideout was shrouded by trees and overgrowth, blending in perfect with the landscape. Most people would never notice it, despite it being on the main path. The door was broken and the walls were falling apart. The roof was intact, except it had several holes that let in plenty of water.

With a wave to the thief, Kestus followed Jeret into the shack without hesitation. The small space smelt of mold and wet leather. Kestus didn't mind. He was ready for a lifetime of respite. If Jeret vouched for the shack, then that meant it was as safe as it could be, and being able to stop for a moment was a blessing, even if it was spent in a rundown place like this.

Pulling an old lantern from a nail on the door. Jeret gave it a good shake before setting it at the center of a large round table and lit it. Then he grabbed a chair and gave it a little brushing before he plopped down hard in the seat.

"Alright, let's see the damned thing…"

CHAPTER 14

The Ties That Bind

"Put it away." Jeret spoke, his head down.

Kestus pulled his shirt sleeve back over the bracer and slumped against the decaying wall of the safehouse. The artifact trembled like his heartbeat, reminding him that he now carried a burden too powerful for any one man.

Jeret stood near the doorway now, his arms crossed, his usual smirk absent. "We've got to get that thing to Tyven," he grumbled, his voice hard and serious. "Kes-Quickhand…How are you wearing that thing? Just looking at it made me feel uneasy, like it's looking back with its one grey eye."

"Jeret, we can't just hand this over to Tyven." Kestus shook his head, his fingers tracing the lines of the bracer through the cloth. "You don't know what I saw back in the castle. King Alikhan… he didn't just give this up. There's something tied to this thing—something darker than we know. All those people down there, they're dead. Because of whatever the hell is going on! We can't just give away the one thing that may make sense of what's happening..." Kestus pleaded, unable to keep his voice even.

Jeret's brow furrowed. "I don't care if it's tied to the gods themselves. We made a deal. You get paid when that bracer is in Tyven's hands, and then you can disappear for a while or start a revolt and overthrow the King. I don't fecking care, Quickhand. You're a fool for not trusting more in Tyven. Just know, if you try to keep that you will have every gang and guard in Tare'Envel breathing down your neck." Jeret turned to Kestus, rubbing his eyes and then holding his arm carefully as he retook his seat at the table. "Let's say you just get rid of it. What then? There are more eyes on this job than you know. There's nowhere and no one you can give it to other than Starstride."

"It's not about the gold anymore!" Kestus pushed himself off the wall. "Jeret. This bracer—t's dangerous. If it falls into the wrong hands, we could see much worse than just the gangs fighting over territory." Thinking about his next words carefully, Kestus fixed Jeret with a stare. "Tyven the Blade could be as dangerous as the King. You know better than I, how exactly he earned the name 'the Blade'. He could sell the bracer to the highest bidder or keep it and use it for whatever twisted plan he's got. The power this thing has is too great. If you saw what it was capable of you would understand."

Jeret's eyes focused on the bracer beneath Kestus' sleeve, a glint of temptation in them. "And you think you're better than him? You just want to keep it for yourself, don't you?" A low growl rumbled in his chest. "Don't be feckin foolish!"

The tension between them was rising. Kestus could feel it, he tried to keep his voice steady, with little success.

"I don't want it, Jeret! No one should have this. Not me, not Tyven and definitely not King Alikhan. We need to be smart. We need to figure out how to destroy it. Or hide it somewhere no one will ever find it. This thing is too powerful."

Jeret sighed long and hard, rubbing the back of his neck. "Fine." He lifted a hand to prevent Kestus from speaking any further. "Kes, I've heard what you have to say. We'll lay low for now and I'll think on your proposition. However! Tyven won't let this slide and it would be both our heads if I agree to help you with this. So give me a moment. I need to consider the alternative risk of me *betraying* Starstride. The gang I am bloodsworn to. The gang I have sweated for, lied for, and bled for."

"Jeret...thank you."

"Sure. Now shut up." With his one good elbow on the table, Jeret put his head to his fist and clinched his eyes tight before lifting one finger into the air. "Tell me this, Kestus Retchet. Why'd you take the job to begin with?" When Jeret looked at Kestus, his eyes bore into him, searching for something. "You were doing well for yourself. You are a named man and you're not even in a fecking gang. I was nearly twice your age before I got mine and it was after being bloodbound for close to two decades. What are you missing? I know you said it's not for the coin, so then...what's all this for? Look at me. I'm sitting here with a damn broken arm. Shite. If not gold, then what? Prestige? Men? Women? A chance at a fathers pride? I don't fecking see it."

Leaning against the wall, his arms crossed, Kestus didn't say anything.

The two men settled into an uneasy silence, their decision hanging over them.

Outside, the city of Tare'Envel continued its restless dance, the sounds of distant footsteps and hushed voices from the courtyard, a constant reminder of the danger lurking just beyond the weathered door.

The safehouse was barely standing. Its walls, leaning like a drunk after a hard day. The roof riddled with gaps, let in the cold morning air as night finally ticked away. For now, it was hidden, and in Tare'Envel's Undercity, that was all one could hope for.

Sliding down, Kestus sat on his heels, tracing the bracer, still feeling each subtle jolt it sent through his body. He knew Jeret was right in one sense —holding onto it would only bring them more trouble. Still, giving it to Tyven? That felt like handing over a loaded crossbow to someone with a finger already on the trigger. The Starstride leader was a great man but you only gain power in Tare'Envel by spilling blood.

"I'll take it to him," Jeret succumbed, his voice breaking the silence. "I wasn't fully honest with you, Quickhand. Feck, I rarely am. It's the nature of the bloody business. Nothing personal. You just can't go around telling thugs and thieves all the sensitive details." That smile Jeret was so well known for peaked out, just as he said the name.

"Lord Rhyden Tuo."

Hardly acknowledging he even heard Jeret, Kestus said nothing.

Clearly waiting for more of a reaction from Kestus, Jeret continued. "Lord Rhyden Tuo, is the backer for the job. He got with Tyven and hired Starstride for the big score, who hired RavenHood for the intel, and that's when I hired you for the heist."

Kestus had never been wronged by Tyven. On the

contrary, every time Kestus had met or seen Tyven, he had only seen the best of the man. However, no one in Tare'Envel trusted Lord Rhyden Tuo. If Tyven was working for him, then that reinforced his belief that Tyven clearly didn't know how drastic this situation was.

There's a chance Tyven doesn't know what he agreed to. I didn't know what would happen when I took this job.

Lord Rhyden Tuo was a noble of nobles. He had wealth to rival King Alikhan's. Rumors circulated the High City, and Undercity of the assassinations he had arranged, pay offs, bribes, anything one could dream of, Lord Rhyden Tuo has perpetrated it. He was the exact kind of person Kestus would not want the Shiftscape Bracer to go to.

"Quickhand, Starstride has the largest gang in the Undercity. You—we, need that sort of protection with what you're talking about. Knife Point, the Hushed, psychopaths and murderers. Who knows if RavenHood is involved too. But Rhyden and that ironclad guardian of his…There's too much uncertainty." Jeret pulled out a rolled slip of tobacco from his coat. "Yep. The only certainty," Jeret pulled out a match and with thumb and forefinger ignited it before lighting the stick. Then with a long drag he continued holding the smoke in his mouth. "Tyven protects his own. You give me the bracer, I'll take it to Tyven and you'll have our protection. You won't even have to join. You continue to do you and live on the outskirts." Jeret released the remaining smoke in a gust from his nostrils. "Feck, you've done other jobs in the past that most seasoned thieves couldn't do, you're already an honorary member. If you want to be a full member, you ought to be. Damn kid, you should be."

Kestus nodded. Clearly seeing Jeret's perspective even if he didn't fully agree with him, Kestus wasn't blind.

"Jeret, I'm not taking off the-"

CHAPTER 15

The Silent Scream

Before Kestus could finish, the door exploded with a deafening crack! Splintered wood flew through the air. Dark figures flooded into the room—silent, swift, and terrifying.

The Hushed had found them.

Kicking off the table, Jeret knocked the lantern to the floor. He leapt to his feet, one hand covering his face from the dust that hung in the air. Dagger drawn, he lunged at the nearest figure. His blade sliced through air, unsure if he missed or if it just sliced through the Hushed like smoke. Jeret staggered back, disbelief etched on his face.

"Fecking bastards!" he swore, slashing again and again at each of the Hushed.

Each attack was futile. The Hushed didn't seem to be affected by steel. Their ghostly shapes closed in with unnerving fluidity.

Already on his feet, Kestus watched as Jeret's dagger moved through each of the invaders, unable to comprehend how they were unharmed. The Hushed moved like shadows, twisting and warping as if they weren't entirely part of this world. If Kestus didn't know better, it was as if they were Shadow Stepping.

More of them poured in, their white cloaks making shadows dance like fire in the light of the broken lantern. Silent and relentless they circled Jeret.

Eyes wide, Jeret turned to Kestus, a look that chilled him to the bone. This was different from the usual scrapes he found himself in—this was a nightmare. Jeret's mouth opened, but no words came out, only terror. A silent scream.

Then, one of the Hushed stepped forward, towering above Jeret. Its hooded form loomed above the man. Its presence drained the air from the room. The room seemed to settle just as it slowly reached up and pulled back its veil.

Kestus' stomach churned at the sight.

The Hushed had no lower jaw. Where a mouth should have been, there was only twisted bone, with hanging flesh like tendrils curling from its exposed throat. Hollow eyes stared out from sunken sockets, their gaze piercing through Jeret like ice.

Stumbling back, Jeret's face drained of color. He mouthed something, a final curse or prayer. Before he could do anything else, the jawless Hushed tilted its head back and opened its mouth—or what remained of it.

A scream erupted from the creature, a sound no living thing should make. It was a distortion of reality itself—a low-pitched, unnatural gurgle that reverberated through the room, shaking the walls and vibrating the air. The sound bypassed Kestus' ears and drove straight into his mind, an agonizing wail that tore at his sanity.

Jeret's body jerked violently as the scream pierced every part of him. His skin rippled, as if an unseen force was filling his body from the inside and forcing itself out, tearing him apart. His eyes locked with Kestus' one final time, filled with horror and regret—and then, in an instant, he was gone.

Jeret's form disintegrated, tissue and muscle shredded into a cloud of dust, scattering through the air in a crimson mist.

The Hushed pulled up its veil, its robes unmarked by the fog of blood and sinew.

Kestus' breath caught in his throat as the drops of his friend painted the walls. His heart raced as the room closed in around him, the Hushed moving closer, their veiled gazes upon him. His legs felt weak, his vision began to darken. The Hushed crowded the shack, slipping into every corner, filling where Jeret had been.

Then the Shiftscape Bracer sent a surge of energy through Kestus. His survival instincts kicked in. Without thinking, he Shadow Stepped.

The world stopped around him, except this time it was different.

Panic flooded through Kestus' veins as the air grew still, suffocating in its stillness. The pale shift between dusk and dawn that filtered through the cracked walls seemed to dim. The faint creak of the broken wooden beams overhead froze, leaving only the hollow thrum of his own heartbeat pounding in his ears.

The shadows in the room swelled unnaturally, growing deeper, darker, as if they were responding to his Shadow Step. Every edge and corner of the safehouse was engulfed by a void-like haze, the dilapidated walls were barely discernible. Yet, amidst the consuming darkness, one thing became clear—something was very wrong.

Eyes darting to the Hushed, Kestus realized with a sinking dread that they were unaffected by the slowing of time. But something else was happening to them, their robes, once immaculate symbols of power and status, hung in filthy tatters, stained a sickly brown. The fabric barely clung to their emaciated forms, their bony frames twisted and contorted as though their bodies had long abandoned any semblance of humanity. Their movements were unsettlingly smooth, almost fluid, as they glided forward.

Unlike everything else in the room, the Hushed cast no shadows. The flickering light of the suspended lantern didn't so much as bend around them; it simply stopped, consumed entirely by their presence. It was as if they didn't belong in this world, their existence defying the laws of reality.

Outside, the safehouse's decrepit surroundings warped under the influence of Kestus' Shadow Step. The overgrown trees that shrouded the shack loomed in the still air, their branches casting impossibly long, claw-like shadows on the ground. The puddles that had collected in the uneven cobblestones outside were still as ice, their surfaces a foggy shimmer as if hiding something. Even the rats that had been scurrying through the damp outside were frozen mid-stride, their claws suspended above the ground.

Kestus' breaths came shallow and labored, each one feeling heavier than the last. The Shiftscape Bracer pulsed, sending vibrations through his arm. His muscles burned as though the bracer was sapping his strength, forcing him to remain within this distorted reality.

"What the hell are you things?" he hissed, his voice trembling as he tried to take a step back.

The Hushed moved as one, their hollow eyes fixed on him, their skeletal frames jerking unnervingly toward his voice. They made no sound, no breath, no shuffling of feet. Only the soft sway of their tattered robes marked their motion.

Instinctively, Kestus reached for his dagger, only to realize it was gone. His hand hovered uselessly in the air, his fingers twitching as the situation pressed down on him.

"Feck," he muttered, under his breath, lowering his hand in resignation.

He didn't want to admit it before, however, this job had proven to be beyond his capabilities, even still he hadn't anticipated this—a confrontation with something that felt more nightmare than reality. He wouldn't rot in a gaile or hang from the gallows; no, his end would be far worse.

As the Hushed closed in, his fingers brushed against something cool and smooth at his side. He looked down and saw the *dagger* he had taken from King Alikhan's vault, its ornate hilt glinting faintly in the distorted light. The intricate runes etched into the blade seemed to glow faintly, pulsing with a rhythm that matched the bracer's.

Gripping the dagger tightly, Kestus drew it from his belt. The weight of it in his hand was both foreign and familiar, a perfect balance that filled him with a sense of control. He raised it, the edge catching what little light remained in the room, and prepared to face the encroaching Hushed.

CHAPTER 16

Tethers

All was still.

The oppressive silence hung in the air as Kestus held the dagger aloft, its green shard casting an eerie glow across the warped interior of the shack. The Hushed had stopped advancing. Their hollow skulls tilted unnaturally toward the blade, the faint green light reflecting in the dark voids where their eyes should have been. The shard, embedded in the ornate hilt of the dagger, radiated, almost as if it were alive.

Before, the shard had appeared inert—a hollowed out emerald. Now, it seemed charged with something far more profound, an essence that exuded awareness. It was similar to the Shiftscape Bracer, but it carried a different encumbrance. Where the bracer pulled at Kestus like a leech feeding on his energy, the dagger connected to everything around it. This wasn't just a weapon; it was an anchor, binding him to the strange, distorted reality surrounding him.

Kestus' breaths came faster, and his lungs strained in the thick, suffocating air of the *Shadow Realm*. Each inhale felt like pulling tar into his chest, and every exhale felt as if bile were stuck in his throat, slowly burning through his skin. He forced himself to focus, swallowing his pain, using the momentary pause to calm his racing heart.

He took a hesitant step forward.

The entire shack seemed to ripple in response. Every one of the Hushed mirrored his movement, hopping back in perfect unison. Their silence was unnerving, yet their retreat sparked a glimmer of hope.

They're afraid of the dagger.

Gripping the hilt tighter, he raised the blade higher, letting its green light flare brighter. The Hushed recoiled further, their thin figures shuddering as though the dagger's presence burned them. Taking another step, then another, Kestus pushed through the viscous air, carving his way toward the doorway.

The world outside flickered, a faint reminder of the normalcy that awaited him. He could see his path through the Hushed—a narrow corridor opening just wide enough for him to escape. His pulse quickened.

Summoning every ounce of strength, Kestus lunged forward. The dagger in his hand cut through the tension like a beacon, forcing the Hushed to part as he sprinted between them. Their decayed forms jerked aside, their tattered robes brushing against him like cold whispers of death.

The moment he crossed the threshold, Kestus released his Shadow Step.

The world roared back into focus.

Rain came crashing down in torrents, each droplet striking him like tiny needles. The sound of the storm was deafening, and the wind howled with enough force to make him stagger. The once stifling air now felt keen and alive, filling his lungs in great gasps as he steadied himself against the onslaught.

Behind him, the Hushed remained at the doorway, their silent forms watching. The jagged edges of their tattered robes reformed, and their ethereal glow returned. They looked pristine once more, their decay hidden, their movements unnervingly graceful.

Kestus didn't dare glance back. He couldn't. The sight of them, still and unrelenting, would steal his courage and leave him frozen. He clenched his teeth and strode forward, his boots splashing against the rain-soaked cobblestones.

Each stride felt harder than the last, the burden of the Shiftscape Bracer on his wrist was a grim reminder of the cost Jeret had paid. The price they both might still pay if he failed to keep running.

The winding streets of Tare'Envel stretched endlessly before him, the Undercity's darkened alleys and crumbling structures swallowing him whole. The distant cries of the city's denizens, muffled by the storm, seemed a world away.

His thoughts turned to Jeret. The devastating reality of what had happened bore down on him. After what he had just faced, nowhere in the city— or outside of it—felt safe. The Hushed would find him. The bracer would ensure that.

Kestus needed protection, and only one name came to mind: Tyven.

The Starstrider had promised safety, and at this moment, that promise was the only thing keeping Kestus moving.

CHAPTER 17

The Seventh Star

The city of Tare'Envel stretched before Kestus. A city he once knew every part of, now it felt as if the city held secrets that could alter the entire world.

Maybe it always did. I was just too blind to notice

As he navigated the twisting streets and alleys toward the Starstride stronghold, the recent events continued to press heavily on him. The loss of Jeret, the looming mystery of Lord Rhyden Tuo, and the question of how he would get Tyven to help him without giving up the bracer, were ever present concerns.

The stormy clouds above mirrored the turmoil within Kestus' mind. The Shiftscape Bracer on his wrist hummed intermittently, its unsettling energy a constant nagging of the mess he was entangled in. He had managed to escape the Hushed, however, last night's events had taken its toll on him.

As he neared the Starstride's territory, Kestus stripped off his guard's uniform and tried to use the cloth on the inside to wipe his face. Since the drainage tunnel, he had been wearing the grime and muck of his journey.

The heart of the market district was where Starstride had their hideout. This part of the Undercity was marked by older, fortified buildings and an air of vigilance. Starstriders patrolled the streets here, making sure no one got too close to their treasures.

Kestus approached the entrance of the stronghold —a tavern—named, *the Seventh Star.*

To the untrained eye, it was just another dingy bar, yet for those in the know, it was the nerve center of the Starstride operations.

I need to be as convincing as the Smile would be, or more people will die. No pressure...

With a deep breath, Kestus pushed through the wooden door.

The tavern was well lit, the smell of ale mingling with the smoky haze of tobacco. The patrons, a mix of burly men and wary women, paid Kestus little attention, or so it seemed. Their eyes only briefly flickered toward him before returning to their conversations. Except, Kestus could see hands move toward daggers at hips or a pant trouser slide up to reveal a blade waiting to be pulled. The Starstride gang were always watchful, their vigilant eyes hidden behind casual glances. Kestus knew how he looked, he just had to hope that his appearance wouldn't cause too much trouble.

Watching me like stars in the sky.

Blood and bone dust stained his pants. Luckily, his undershirt was only smudged with rain and sweat. He had wrapped his uniform inside out around his wrist, concealing the bracer. Ensuring the dirtiest part of the guard uniform was the only part that was revealed, in hope, no one would confuse him for a castle guard.

A few faces recognized him. No one smiled, however, he could see a couple from the crowd give him a welcoming nod. Nodding back, Kestus made his way to the bar, where the barkeep—a tall man with a distinctive scar running down his neck —gave him a brief once over and then gestured toward the back room.

A staircase led Kestus up to the second floor. He moved down a narrow hallway, no wider than if three people stood shoulder to shoulder, the walls had an old wallpaper with a subtle floral pattern depicting a rose garden. The transition from tavern to a traditional decor caught Kestus off guard.

Tyven must have a gentle side.

The hallway led to a guarded door. Two men stood watch; one broad-shouldered with a shaved head and the other was forgettable, a useful trait in Tare'Envel. The bald man stepped forward as Kestus approached.

"State your business," the guard ordered. A tad too blunt for Kestus' liking.

"I need to see Tyven," Kestus replied, meeting the guard's gaze. "It's urgent."

The guard's expression hardened. "Tyven doesn't see just anyone. So say more, or scurry on little rat. We don't need a stench like you hanging around."

The bracer pulsed. Picking up on Kestus' thoughts, it wanted him to use his Shadow Step, to show this thug he was no better than the Knife Point gang he had beat down.

"He'll see me," Kestus insisted. "Tell him Quickhand is here. He'll want to hear what I have to say."

The guard scrutinized Kestus for a moment before knocking on the door.

"I got Quickhand here. The Smile's not with him." The bald man called through the door.

It creaked open just wide enough for Kestus to

slip inside. The bald man grunted, clearly annoyed by the thief's appearance, but stepped out of the way. Kestus' heart raced as he entered, ignoring the guards, unsure of what awaited him.

CHAPTER 18

A Seat at the Table

As Kestus entered, a murmur swept through the room. The Starstride members' expressions shifted from grim to surprised and even some looked relieved.

The room was much larger than expected. Ornate oil lamps lit the room, casting a royal light. A redwood table dominated the space, around which several Starstride members, lieutenants and named men were seated in fine leather chairs. At the head of the table sat Tyven, the leader of Starstride.

Tyven was an imposing figure even sitting down, his scarred face and commanding presence gave him an air of authority. His dark brown eyes made every expression look thoughtful and calculating, reflecting the strategic brilliance for which he was known. He was a legacy story. Started a beggar, an orphan of the Undercity, who rose through the ranks, distinguishing himself with a sword, and one day head of the gang. There were dozens of stories of how he fought, stole, and tricked people to get to his spot.

The Blade. Somehow you look a noble in a room of thieves and cutthroats.

A sudden voice brought Kestus back from his thoughts.

"Quickhand? You're alive!" One member he didn't recognize rejoiced. A man that looked to be the same age as himself. He wore a Starstride cloak, the stars woven in the hood clearly distinguishing him, yet Kestus couldn't place him.

Maybe he was with Jeret's group? He's not someone I can remember, and I can place nearly everyone here.

"I thought you were done for!" another added. Pouch Grabber, her name was. "I was with Smile when them pricks came looking around for you."

Tyven's gaze was cool and curious. "Kestus Quickhand." His voice was low, the others in the room went silent. "I'm glad to see you have survived the chaos." Peering around the table he gave a few looks to some of the members. Understanding the sensitive nature, they rose from the table and left the room. Stepping past Kestus.

Moving further into the room, Kestus saw a bottle

of malt liquor and poured himself a drink. The taste made him wince, as it burned the cuts in his mouth he didn't know he had.

"You have no idea." Kestus grimaced, through gritted teeth.

Tyven raised an eyebrow. He waited for the door to shut before he continued.

"Here is what I know. I have heard rumors about a heist gone awry causing the castle to lock its gates. No one in or out. Knife Point has broken the treaty and crossed into our territory unbidden. We have already sent striders to deal with multiple incursions. What really worries me, is I have heard stories of the Hushed appearing throughout the Undercity. Their intentions, still shrouded in mystery. I would like to make sense of this catastrophe. As you were at the center of it all, please enlighten me."

Kestus glanced around at the remaining Starstride members, his gaze falling lastly on Tyven.

"I need your help,"

"Where is Jeret?" Tyven asked, as if he didn't hear Kestus.

Kestus took a deep breath.

"Jeret is dead."

Tyven leaned in closer, his expression unreadable. Yet, Kestus saw the twitch. A small squint of the right eye. That's what Kestus neede to see, if this man was too callous to react to his friend's death, he would've known there was no trusting Tyven. However, that small twitch, the faintest acknowledgment of pain—that was something he understood.

Taking another glance at the liquor, Kestus turned away from it and took an empty seat at the table. Unraveling his shirt, he revealed the Shiftscape Bracer.

A brief intake of breath from a few members broke the silence.

"You have it..." Tyven's eyes widened. The look on his scarred face was of pure disbelief, and still Kestus felt he could see something deeper. A look of regret and maybe resignation?

With a nod, Kestus began recounting the events since the heist. He described the underground cathedral, the King's bloody ritual, Knife Point's ambush. He spoke of Jeret's death at the hand of the Hushed—deliberately leaving out the parts that involved his Shadow Step and the stolen dagger. To his own ears, his story seemed unreal.

Listening intently, Tyven did not betray any more of his emotions. When Kestus finished, no one said a word. The room was quiet enough to hear the noise of the bar below. People were chatting, glasses clinking or thudding on tables—a building of people ignorant and unaware of what was happening beyond these four walls.

"Just before he died, Jeret told me that the benefactor of all this...was *Lord Rhyden Tuo?*" Kestus whispered.

The final statement brought out a sigh from Tyven. Eyes on the table the man collected his thoughts before speaking.

"Yes." Knitting his fingers and placing his elbows on the table, Tyven looked at Kestus dead on, his stare piercing. A few of the others in the room shifted in their seats.

It looks like I'm not the only who didn't know that.

"Lord Tuo, came to me with a request. To steal from the King, a treasure so grand, it held the power to cause a war. A treasure so powerful that it would bring blood to the streets of Tare'Envel, if left in Alikhan's selfish grip. This heist—this job...it was meant to prevent that possibility, it was never meant to be the catalyst of it all." Getting to his feet, Tyven moved to stand in front of a window that looked out upon the back alley.

"If Rhyden knows about the Shiftscape Bracer then he must know about King Alikhan's ritual! I need to know. Tyven, do you have any idea of what he wants it for?" Kestus had his hands on the table, his fingers quietly tapping.

Placing his fists behind his back, Tyven turned to look at Kestus, his face firm. Kestus guessed Tyven wasn't used to having to answer to anyone, especially not a boundless thief.

"Not in the least. He summoned me to his manor, where he and his ironclad guardian proceeded to inform me of the Shiftscape artifact. They emphasized the power it possessed. I did inquire about how he had come by this information. Sir Tuo only laughed at my request. He then spoke of the urgency of the job and how it needed to happen quickly. He had told us that it would be transported elsewhere, now we know he actually wanted it before King Alikhan could enact the ritual. However, from your tale, it appears as if we were too late." Walking to his chair, Tyven placed his arms across the high leather back.

Exhaustion setting in, Kestus sat back in his seat. "Is there anything else Rhyden may have said? Nothing more about the Shiftscape Bracer?"

"Beyond the dramatics, he did not offer any further details of what he wanted to do with the Shiftscape Bracer, nor did he mention the ritual." Turning his gaze back outside, Kestus saw Tyven regain his heir of authority. He stood straighter, almost at attention. "This was not a normal job, the weight he pressed upon me of the havoc that would ensue was worth the risk, or so I believed." Leaving one hand behind his back, Tyven clinched his other into a fist in front of him. "We need to ensure that the bracer does not get back to the King, or we all will pay in blood."

"The bracer—it's dangerous. We can't just give it to some other noble because you made a deal with him. Tyven, you know better than most, the politics High City nobles fight over mean nothing but hardship and pain for the Undercity. Rhyden may take the bracer and do exactly what the King is trying to do or maybe something even worse!"

"Quickhand, I understand your concern." Tyven's eyes narrowed, and with a pause he refocused his thoughts. "However, you must remember, you sit in my council. Do not continue to speak to me in this manner. You are my guest." The words and the threat hung there. "We all know of Rhyden. The deviant noble, with their hand in everyone's pocket. Quickhand, most of the rumors about him are paid gossip—exaggerated to scare off those who might challenge him. To create fear of him in the court, to keep the King on edge and wary of his competitor. We, Starstride, are some of the major distributors of these falsehoods. Of course, that is not common knowledge. While his motives are not known to me, they do not frighten me. As someone familiar with King Alikhan and his court, Lord Rhyden Tuo is exactly who we need to be sitting there." Clearing his throat, he continued. "Startstride does not go back on our deals. I will deliver the Shiftscape Bracer to him, with or without you. However, I would prefer your assistance." The tension of the room changed with Tyven's words. Kestus' hair on his arms rose as if lighting were about to strike. Tyven's free hand now rested on the hilt of a dagger at his hip.

Others in the room, previously statues, now shifted —mirroring Tyven's threat. Pouch Grabber had her knife, a small thin dagger with a star notched in its hilt, laying on the table in front of her. Their eyes met and she blew a kiss at him.

Kestus clenched his fists. "If Rhyden gets his hands on this thing, it could mean death for us all. The things I saw tonight..." Kestus took a steadying breath. "It's the beginning of something bigger. Something worse. We need to gather everyone we can to try and stop it. We can't just give up the one thing we know that everyone wants."

Rubbing his scarred eye, Tyven gave a pained smile. "Rhyden already has the means to destroy Starstride, with or without the Shiftscape Bracer. By fulfilling the bargain, we align ourselves with a powerful ally. King Alikhan continues to reveal himself to be an unknown threat, and we need to prepare but we can not alienate ourselves in the process. We must trust one another."

He turned to his crew, scanning their faces. "Are we all of the same mind?"

Pouch Grabber, was the first to speak, "Bound in blood, now and until my final stride through the stars."

"Here here." Another spoke, and then a collective gathering of agreement rippled through the group.

"Marvelous." With a final glance at Kestus, Tyven nodded as if to say there will be no further discussion. "We need to prepare. We know where Knife Point is, and need to make it top priority to minimize the damage. If they are in league with the Hushed or Alikhan, we can expect that they will be far more dangerous now they think they have support. Do not engage them, if it can be avoided. We need to be smart and take care of our people. Any loss of life is like a falling star, the night will only grow darker. Quickhand's story confirms our fear of the Hushed and their strange abilities, it is better not to battle with a foe we cannot defeat. Make sure everyone knows to run at first sight of them, yet be sure to mark their whereabouts. We need to piece together their role in all this."

Kestus watched as the remaining members rose immediately and moved into action, their faces set with grim determination. He moved slowly and tried to hold the bracer inconspicuously. When he noticed Pouch Grabber approached with a smile.

"I wasn't really going to stab you, I just like the drama. Maybe next time, you can give me some pointers though, Quickhand." She bent low and gave him a kiss on the cheek, her hand resting on his shoulder just longer than a second before she rushed off.

Tyven's response was pragmatic, and Kestus knew what Tyven had said made sense, still he knew that the Starstrider was wrong. No one knew the bracer's power, no one except for him, and it would be his decision if he would part with it.

As the final Starstrider left and the door shut, Tyven walked over and sat in the chair next to Kestus. "Now I want you to tell me everything you know about the bracer and what it is actually capable of."

"I told you-"

"Kestus, I know you left out details. Please. We need to be ready and if what you say is true... How can we use the Shiftscape Bracer to help us? You have survived things no ordinary person could have, Jeret believed the same. And I know it is because of the power you carry on your wrist." Leaning in, Tyven gripped the arms of Kestus' chair.

Kestus didn't expect this sudden change in Tyven.

This wasn't the confident leader holding a whole city together, this was a man afraid of the destruction he had inadvertently brought to his people.

"I see the effects this artifact has had on your body, Quickhand. You are barely holding your head up. That kind of exhaustion comes from tapping your reserves and pushing yourself even harder than your body can take."

Trying to pull further from the man, Kestus' throat grew dry. Jeret trusted Tyven, and Kestus trusted Jeret. The Starstride's aid would be crucial in preventing whatever was coming. He would have to be honest in order for them to work together.

"You're right. I might have left out a few details." Tyven let go of the chair and sat back as Kestus began to speak. "Some of this is going to sound unbelievable, but I swear on Porox's tongue, everything is true..."

CHAPTER 19

Dying Star

Just as Kestus began to elaborate on the details of the Shiftscape Bracer, the bustling of the inn below became a frantic clamoring. A sudden crash echoed from the lower floor of the tavern, followed by a cacophony of shouts and the clattering of metal.

The Seventh Star was under attack.

Kestus' heart pounded in his chest. He exchanged a worried glance with Tyven, whose face had darkened with a grim realization.

"Damn it all!" Tyven shouted. He rushed to the wall and ripped a sword from the crossed blades mounted above the bar, shattering their careful symmetry. They had been hung there to be remembered, not to be used.

Kestus' breath came faster, more strained, as he started to panic that it was the Hushed again. He couldn't escape them, no matter where he went. There was no way he could Shadow Step again, Tyven was right, he was spent. There were no reserves to draw from. This would be it. The ghouls would kill him this time.

Clenching his eyes shut, Kestus shook, trying not to remember the puff of mist that Jeret had become, the scream that rippled through Jeret's body, the face of the creature beneath the veil…

"Kestus." A hand gingerly rested upon his shoulder —bringing the thief out of his nightmare. Meeting Tyven's eyes, Kestus eased. No words were said, and still he knew Tyven would do everything he could to protect him.

I should have come here sooner. Maybe then, maybe Jeret would be standing here with us.

Upon his shoulder, now lay a cloak of Starstride blue, deep and dark like the night sky, with faint gray lining. Rising to his feet, Kestus dawned the gift with a flourish. The cloak fit perfectly, even better than his old one.

Feeling the fabric in his hand, Kestus' mind wondered again. "I hope the spy got out."

"She did. Ellia grabbed her before the castle got locked down and sent the girl to let us know that you had continued on. She held a tattered cloak and refused to give it up, even when Pouch Grabber ensured she would get it back to you. You must have left a real impression on that little one." There was a hint of a smile before Tyven returned his focus to what was happening below.

Finding the hilt of his stolen dagger, Kestus pushed away his fear and doubt. If it were the Hushed, he could deal with them, the dagger was all he needed. Still Kestus couldn't ignore the pull to the Shiftscape Bracer. The bracer craved to be used. That craving made Kestus realize this was his opportunity. He could show Tyven the bracer's power, and show him that it wasn't something to be traded away. Kestus would just have to push himself one more time to do it.

I can do it one more time.

The two men, both filled with purpose, gave each other a final nod and strode from the back room together.

- - - - - - - - -

The door from the tavern had been broken down, the bald guard that had been watching the door was fending off a small group of Knife Points that had tried rushing the hallway, alone. The thugs were obscured by masks and their weapons glinted in the hallway light.

With a glance to Kestus, Tyven leapt forward.

There was no hesitation in the man's step. This was his crew, his home, his territory. If anyone tried to take it from him, they would have to taste the steel of his blade first.

Trailing a few feet behind, Kestus was taken aback by the precision in Tyven's movements. With a false step, Tyven tricked one of the thugs to step forward, allowing the bald Starstrider to jab a club into the Knife Point's stomach, just as Tyven got close enough to run his blade across the Knife Point's throat and in the same movement, whip his blade and pierce through the neck of the second thug.

The two Knife Point lackeys were down before Kestus ever caught up.

This is why he is known as the Blade.

"Knife Point dogs." The bald man spat on the dead men. Tyven offered the guard his handkerchief. A gash bled from the side of the bald man's head, the majority of his left ear had been cut off. If he wasn't a named man before, Kestus thought he would be after today.

"Where's Rowe?" Tyven asked.

The bald man pointed at a corpse down the stairs, behind the shattered door. "There…"

Tyven frowned. "Guard these stairs, Allurd. Do not

let anyone pass." He shot Kestus a quick glance, readied his sword, and cautiously continued down the stairs.

"I will do my duty, until my final stride through the stars." Kestus heard the bald man, Allurd, repeat this over and over as he followed Tyven down the blood stained stairs. He readied himself for what was to come and clutched his dagger tight.

The simple inn was transformed into a battlefield. Bodies from both sides lay scattered across broken tables and chairs, light from the sunrise flooded in the gaping hole, where the front door had once stood vigilant, it was now splinters spread beneath boots.

Knife Point outnumbered the Starstriders two to one. Their leader cut through the chaos with roared orders, his presence fierce and commanding. Kestus recognized him immediately, the broken-nosed thug from when he escaped the castle.

"Maybe I didn't teach you a clear enough message," Kestus growled, rushing the brute.

As the Starstriders scrambled, chaos took hold. Screams echoed and blades rang out, but Kestus stayed focused. Tyven could manage the rest. The leader was Kestus's concern—he had faced him before and won.

The Knife Point leader caught sight of the thief and

with a grin he started to move towards him.

The confidence Kestus had slowly slipped away as the jolts of his steps reignited the pain from his ribs. The space between the two men started to disappear quickly. With a quick glance at his feet, he maneuvered around a body on the floor and when he looked back up, Broken Nose was there sword in hand.

"Rahhhh!" The man's veins popped from his neck and forehead with his scream. "I will kill you for what you did to me!"

"Not good!" Eyes wide, Kestus braced himself as the pommel of Broken Nose's sword bashed him squarely in the chest.

The body Kestus had carefully stepped over cushioned his fall as he plummeted to the floor. The impact sent all the air from his lungs and for a few brief gasps, Kestus didn't think it would ever be possible to catch his breath. The room spun, he no longer could tell which direction he was facing. Then a hand gripped his shoulder and helped pull him to his feet.

"Thank you," Kestus wheezed between gasped breaths, hoping it was a friend and not Broken Nose.

When his vision finally focused, Kestus watched a figure glide across the other end of the room, Tyven was in a clash of swords. Two people attacked him, a woman with a halberd on one side and a man with a dagger in each hand from the other.

Only the King's guard wields halberds. Is Knife Point being armed by the King? What the feck is going on.

As Kestus pondered, his gaze turned to the hand still resting on his shoulder. His had forgotten in his stupor..

Pay attention! You're in a fecking battle.

Expecting to see Tyven looking back at him, Kestus remembered that the swordmaster was amidst a deadly confrontation, meaning there was no possible way this hand could belong to him. When his eyes finally fell upon the crooked nose of Broken Nose, Kestus felt his body go numb.

Broken Nose had his sword ready. The blade stood poised—eager to pierce flesh.

Feck.

Resigning to his fate, Kesrus sighed and closed his eyes, just as a clang reverberated through his body.

Eyes darting open, Kestus had to catch his balance as the hand supporting him suddenly ripped away as a familiar face dug a dagger into Broken Nose's shoulder.

"Get moving, Quickhand. I got this one!" The man

called out looking over his shoulder to give Kestus a quick smile.

Still unable to remember his name or place him, Kestus recognized his savior as the man from the table that was relieved to see he was still alive. His smile looked similar to Jeret's.

Did the Smile have a son?

"No! WAIT!" Kestus screamed, lurching forward.

Yanking the dagger from his own shoulder, Broken Nose grasped the man's face, and slammed the blade into the Starstrider's abdomen. Letting the man fall to his knees, Broken Nose took a step back just before he swung his sword into the man's neck.

A thick thunk of metal hitting bone, echoed through Kestus. Gurgles and blood spilled from the Starstrider's mouth, his arms flailing unsure of what to do.

With a quick scan, Kestus picked up the ornate dagger he dropped, the fire inside of him lighting with a scorching fervor.

The world blurred and darkened as Kestus entered his Shadow Step. The air thickened, a suffocating stillness enveloping the room. The glittering lanterns that cast light and shapes across the bloodstained walls now hung frozen, their flames now a static glow. Time had paused, but the atmosphere seemed alive—pulsating like a heartbeat of a beast ready to pounce.

The room distorted in Kestus' vision. Edges of tables, broken chairs, and bodies strewn across the floor seemed stretched and elongated, their forms bending unnaturally as though the Shiftscape Bracer was pulling reality into itself. The blood beneath fallen Starstride members shimmered, suspended in air as if rubies ready to be stolen.

Locked in time, Broken Nose stood with his sword embedded deep in the chest of another Starstride ally. His face was an ugly strain of muscles, veins bulged green and blue, in his neck and hands; a grotesque mask of fury caught mid-yell contorted his features. Around him his remaining thugs were paralyzed in various states of movement—one lunging forward, the other half way through their swing. Every face was twisted with fear and rage, trapped like statues in an ancient tableau.

Gripping his ornate dagger tighter, Kestus could feel his own rage bubble over. Every step he took toward Broken Nose reverberated faintly, a muffled echo in this distorted void. He felt the energy of the bracer surging, an extension of his own fury. Together they could do anything. Clear in his purpose, Kestus approached Broken Nose, the ornate blade glowed faintly, casting jagged green reflections across the brute's face.

With a scream that tore through the suffocating silence, Kestus brought the dagger down. The blade cut cleanly.

The strain in his body began to become unbearable, his lungs burning from the effort of sustaining the Shadow Step.

Bracing himself, Kestus let it go. The room slammed back into normalcy; lantern flames fluttered violently, the sounds of the world roared back, groans of pain from fallen friends and foes rose up like a crescendo, the bang of clashing metal an accompanying tune, and the underlining rhythmic pattern of dripping blood, overwhelmed Kestus' ears.

Falling to his knees, Broken Nose clutched his face, his agonized cries filling the room, scarlet red flowed freely through his fingers and soaked the floor where his nose lay.

Behind Kestus, Tyven dispatched the two thugs with ruthless precision, stepping over their limp bodies as he came to Kestus' side. His eyes moved from the dead Starstriders and then to No Nose, who writhed in pain.

"Dorran will look upon your head as I line the fence with all those who came here today. Knife Point will meet its end at the edge of my blade. There will be no forgiveness for you or Ironfist," Tyven snarled, his voice carrying finality. The Knife Point leader responded with a grin so wide it stretched unnaturally across his bloodied face, a grin even Jeret would have envied.

Something wasn't right. Tyven's eyes narrowed, but the realization nearly came too late.

"Quickhand, look out!" Tyven's voice cut through the chaos. With reflexes honed by countless battles, he lunged toward Kestus, shoving him back with a force that sent the thief sprawling to the floor.

Kestus slammed into the ground, pain exploding through his ribs. Dazed, he looked up just in time to see a pale, thin hand rake the air where his neck had been a heartbeat earlier.

"No, no, no..." he panicked, the words barely audible over the roaring chaos.

From the shadows, they came.

The Hushed emerged like specters from a nightmare, their nearly translucent forms gliding through the air with an unnatural grace. Their veil's were down—still Kestus could feel the hollow spaces where eyes might have been—staring at him. The temperature dropped sharply, the air thick with dread.

"The Hushed!" several screamed, the terror in their voice spreading frenzied terror like wildfire.

Far from retreating, the sight of the Hushed seemed to embolden the remaining Knife Point thugs. Their savagery redoubled as they surged forward, cutting through Starstride's defenses with chilling delight. The coordinated violence of Knife Poin, and the otherworldly presence of the Hushed created a scene of nightmarish carnage.

Adrenaline coursed through Kestus' veins as he scrambled to his feet. The Shiftscape Bracer hummed in sync with his pounding heartbeat, its faint glow blurring the light around it. His fingers brushed the hilt of the ornate dagger, its metal a grounding reassurance in the madness enveloping him.

Tyven fought like a storm, his blade flashing as he felled one Knife Point thug after another. Despite his skill and fury, even he seemed strained under the relentless onslaught.

Kestus tightened his grip on the dagger once more, the cold leather of the hilt steadying him. Gritting his teeth, he whispered to himself. "Let's see if I can pull it off again."

Taking a deep breath and he stepped toward the violence, ready to face whatever came next, his mind racing and his resolve hardening like steel.

Determined, Kesrus thrust his dagger into the air. The dagger sang with his swift movement.

A moment passed and nothing happened. The Hushed were unphased, continuing their assault.

"What the hell are you doing Quickhand? Don't just stand there. Fight!" Tyven shouted, side stepping a grip of the white robed ghouls.

Kicking himself, Kestus moved.

Feck, feck, feck. Why didn't that work!?

Fighting alongside Tyven and what remained of Starstride, Kestus' movements were quick and desperate. Despite their best efforts, the Starstride's stronghold, once a fortress of power and unity, was rapidly falling into disarray. The sounds of combat were deafening, mingled with the moans of the wounded and dying.

Determined to help, Kestus focused on the Shiftscape Bracer. The pull of the bracer soothed his pain as it begged him to use its power once more. Closing his eyes, Kestus took in a deep breath and as he let it out, he let the power of the bracer flow through him. The Shiftscape's energy blended with his Shadow Step, and around him everything stopped.

Shadow filled the room, outlining all that it touched. The faces around him distorted, held in place—agony, fear, joy, terror, Kestus could see a smattering of emotions played out across the devastated tavern. The darkness seemed deeper, like a void ready to consume Tare'Envel. The only light came from the stolen ornate dagger, green threads stretched out, connecting everything and everyone by strings of light to the gem in his dagger. Feeling a healing aura, Kestus was revitalized. With this power coursing through him, he knew what he needed to do.

Kestus moved.

His movements were like the wind, flowing from place to place as if he were a gust himself. He approached the Knife Point thugs, Kestus had never killed before, and despite what the Hushed did to Jeret and what Knife Point had done tonight... he still couldn't bring himself to slay these people.

Still, he had to do something, so he slammed his fist into every single thug's face. He grabbed a club from a boy covered in dirt and grime and smashed elbows holding swords or daggers or spears. None would die at his hand, but he wouldn't forgive them for what they've done and they would remember this night.

Crossing the hall of the Seventh Star, he punched, kicked, and smashed every single Knife Point thug, while being sure to avoid the Hushed. He held his dagger tight, however, they weren't cowering away. Instead they watched him. Unaffected by the Shiftscape Bracer's power, they just stood as if waiting for their moment. Kestus wondered if he had done something different before to control them.

These ones seemed to be different. More aware.

Before, the Hushed morphed from ethereal creatures into beggar-like beings. These were a higher class, they looked to be less withered, their eyes seemed to be burned out, even still, the empty sockets held a knowing presence. A deeper knowing. They didn't flinch at the stolen dagger, the one that had grasped at Kestus seemed to see the thread. It looked down at the string connecting it to the dagger, then it turned and looked out the hole in the wall from where they came from. Kestus squinted and he could see a stream of light similar to his, yet this one was thicker and it was only connected to the Hushed.

Someone else is controlling these monsters…

The power of the bracer began to press on Kestus. His breathing grew heavier, his heart beat harder—the rhythmic thump turning into a struggled thud against his chest. Letting go of his Shadow Step the world had a harsh refocusing. Every Knife Point member screamed as bones broke and weapons fell to the ground. The entire room filled with cries of pain and agony, except this time, Starstride was now in control. At least over Knife Point.

It was then, the Hushed, just like at the safehouse

began flooding the room like a spout left on.

Tyven slashed at the Hushed in front of him, and just as Jeret was, the swordmaster was unable to harm the creatures. Unlike Jeret, Tyven was quicker and more experienced. He placed obstacles in the Hushed's way and made a calculated retreat, placing himself up against Kestus' back, facing the gaping hole where the door to the tavern once stood.

"Whatever you did Quickhand, that was incredible! Now how do we get out of this?" Tyven panted.

In the midst of the chaos, a new figure appeared at the entrance.

"Tyven this way!" The man shouted into the building.

"Great timing. Time to run Quickhand," Tyven yelled, grasping Kestus by the cloak and tugging him along.

Again a hand reached for Kestus, unable to twist away, the thin nearly bone fingers stretched and caressed the skin of his throat. Then, a sound like air being split in two rushed past and the hand of the Hushed departed from its arm. The sword that hung in the space before Kestus dripped a strange kind of blackened blood, the blade gleamed in the tavern light, etched with ancient markings. As his eyes chased the blade to its hilt, the hand holding the blade wasn't that of a thief or thug, but of a noble.

A cuffed sleeve protruded from a black coat inlaid with a purple satin. The coat flowed into a cape-like flap to the man's elegant pitch covered boots. As Kestus' eyes settled on the noble, sharp features marked out the man's face. Long hair pulled into a chonmage, with flowing strands down the sides of his face framed pointed eyebrows, that lead to a pointed nose, and pursed lips. Kestus guessed that this was Lord Rhyden Tuo.

He had come to collect what was his.

CHAPTER 20

A Noble Rescue

Flanked by a figure encased in a suit of armor, Kestus realized he was in the presence of Rhyden's formidable enforcer. The armored figure moved with an unnatural grace, as though the weight of their iron was nothing. They stood taller than anyone else in the room and leapt upon the Hushed with a vigor matching that of a cat hunting a mouse.

Nearby, Lord Rhyden cut through the chaos with a cold, surgical precision. Tyven the Blade was a legend, yet Rhyden fought as if born of war itself. Every strike, every parry, carried an unearthly control, his movements so fluid it seemed as though he had foreseen the battle long before it began. Together, Rhyden and his ironclad guardian pushed back the Hushed and the Knife Point attackers, their presence creating a pocket of calm amidst the carnage.

Rhyden turned to Kestus, his stern face unreadable. "We need to leave. Starstride is lost."

"No, we're w-winning!" Kestus stammered, struggling to process Rhyden's command. "With you two here, we can push them back. These people need us! The Blade, you, your guardian—"

Rhyden's commanding tone cut him off. "No. This fight is already forfeit. We leave."

Before Kestus could argue further, Rhyden turned away. In a motion faster than thought, his blade swept through the neck of a Hushed, the creatures head falling to the ground as Rhyden sheathed his sword. Without a glance at the corpses around him, he strode toward the exit.

"I will not abandon my crew!" Tyven's voice rang with defiance as he moved among the wounded, lifting his men and urging others to follow.

Suddenly, Kestus felt himself shoved forward by the ironclad enforcer, their strength unrelenting, forcing him to walk. The path out of the inn was a gauntlet of blood and bodies, the aftermath of Rhyden and his protector's merciless efficiency.

Pausing, Kestus lingered at the threshold of the Seventh Star, his gaze locked on Tyven. Blood and sweat streaked Tyven's face, his movements fierce and unrelenting as he fought against an unyielding tide of enemies as the stunned Knife Point began to reclaim their weapons and charge forward. The numbers were against him, but he held his ground with a defiance that bordered on madness. Behind him, his men struggled to rise, their battered bodies forming a desperate shield to protect their leader. Even Allurd had abandoned his post to stand beside the Blade,

If this was the end, it didn't matter if he died here or in the hallway to an empty room.

For a moment, their eyes met.

"Quickhand, go!" Tyven roared, his voice barely audible over the cacophony of clashing steel and agonized cries.

Kestus' chest tightened as a war waged within him, every fiber of his being screamed to stay, to fight alongside Tyven and Starstride. The cloak on his back seemed to grow heavier. Yet, reality clawed at his thoughts—Rhyden was right—this battle was lost. Even if they turned the tide here, the Hushed and Knife Point forces would swarm them from every corner of the city. Their numbers were endless, their victory inevitable.

As if daring him to disobey, Tyven's fierce glare burned into him. Still, Kestus couldn't move.

Then, another forceful shove from Rhyden's ironclad enforcer broke his paralysis, sending him stumbling into the acrid morning air.

Out in the open street, Kestus was struck by the full scope of the disaster. The stronghold wasn't just falling—it was burning. Flames licked the edges of buildings, sending thick, acrid smoke into the sky. The air rang with the clamor of steel, the wailes of the wounded, and the distant, chilling howls of the bewildered Knife Point.

The streets were littered with the dead and dying, the last remnants of Starstride fighting desperately in an unwinnable battle. Kestus' breath hitched as he took it all in. Though his mind screamed at him to stop, to stay and fight, his body obeyed the silent command of Rhyden's enforcer, pushing him deeper into the ruined Undercity and further from the raging inferno that had been Starstride's final stand.

The sounds of the Seventh Star's desperate battle faded into the distance as they fled through the narrow streets, shrouded in the smoke and chaos.

Behind him, the rising sun cast a grim light on the burning Undercity, where courage and loyalty clashed against despair and defeat.

CHAPTER 21

Ash and Resolve

The streets of Tare'Envel smoldered with mania. Smoke from the burning market district choked the air, blotting out the morning light and showering ash like filthy snow. Each breath tasted of ruin, the pungent scent of charred wood and flesh clinging to Kestus' nose. The distant echoes of battle lingered, screams and steel carried on the wind replacing the songs of the birds, a bleak reminder that danger was never far behind.

Stopping abruptly, Rhyden turned on Kestus with eyes that pierced like daggers. His presence, even in the haze of destruction, was demanding and unshakable.

"You owe me for this," he remarked, his voice low and unwavering. "And keep up, Theif. Aegis isn't here to save you if you fall behind."

Too tired to respond, Kestus nodded, his breath ragged and uneven. His muscles screamed in protest with every step, his body battered and bruised from the night's ordeal. Still, he forced himself onward, the phantom of Tyven's defiant gaze haunting him. Behind them, the ruins of the Seventh Star loomed. A funeral pyre, its flames threatening to burn down the heavens. The Starstride's fall was stark and absolute—a sobering realization of how quickly power can crumble in Tare'Envel.

Kestus clenched his jaw, forcing down the lump in his throat.

I hope you're okay, Tyven. I'm sorry, I couldn't save you or Jeret...

Cutting through his thoughts, Rhyden's words were like a blade.

"We can't look back. That bracer is too important to lose, now that it's finally in my reach."

Kestus' fists tightened, turning his knuckles white. His chest heaved, both with exhaustion and fury.

"Let me make this clear—I'm coming with you, but the bracer stays with me. This disaster? It's on you."

Spinning on the thief, Rhyden's gaze lingered, his expression unreadable. The tension hung heavy between them, a silent battle of wills. Then, with a measured nod, the noble broke the standoff.

"You're right. I miscalculated, and for that, I apologize." He straightened, his focus shifting to the path ahead. "For now, we head to my manor in the High City. There, we'll have safety. Even Alikhan would not dare cross me on my own ground. There we can discuss what happens next."

The gravity in Rhyden's voice was undeniable, and despite himself, Kestus felt the tension in his chest ease slightly. Still, doubt lingered. Safety felt like a distant memory, and trusting Rhyden was a gamble he couldn't afford to lose.

The trio moved silently through the ash-laden streets, the chaos of the Undercity fading behind them. They passed through alleys where the remnants of the fallen still clung to the walls, the dead and dying scattered like discarded dolls. Buildings once filled with life and laughter now stood hollow, their windows shattered, their frames blackened with soot.

Kestus' boots crunched against broken glass as they approached the district gates. The towering structures of the High City loomed above, their pristine walls unmarred by the destruction below. The contrast between the two worlds gnawed at him, a bitter prick, of how easily the rich and powerful could shield themselves from the suffering they had caused.

Rhyden glanced over his shoulder, his tone softening, though his posture remained unyielding.

"This isn't just about survival, Sir Kestus. It's about reclaiming control. You don't have to trust me fully. Rest assured, you'll understand soon enough why I'm doing this and what we are actually trying to stop.

Saying nothing, Kestus' gaze was fixed on the path ahead. The ash falling around him reminded him of all that he had lost. Allowing the silence between them to grow greater, until it was deafening, he kept his head down and continued on. Each step carried the promise of sanctuary, though the cost of survival was one Kestus could not yet fathom.

CHAPTER 22

The Edge of Revelation

The fire crackled softly in the hearth of Rhyden Tuo's grand manor, its golden light casting long shadows across the lavish room. The dark polished wood gleamed beneath the firelight, and the rich tapestries hanging from the stone walls seemed to shift with the dancing of the flames. It was an environment of wealth and power, a world Kestus had never truly belonged to. He sat uneasily in a plush armchair, his fingers tapping rhythmically on the armrests as his eyes locked on the Shiftscape Bracer lying on the polished table between Rhyden and himself. Its metallic surface blurring faintly, its sleek form barely betraying the immense power it held, like a slumbering dragon ready to awaken.

The significance of everything, the room, the manor, the bracer bore into Kestus. This wasn't just a moment of reflection or conversation—this was the culmination of something vast. The air was thick with unspoken truths, and Kestus felt the tension pulling him deeper into a world he barely understood.

He shifted in his seat, suddenly aware of how bare his arm felt without the bracer strapped to it. Its absence dug into him. It had become more than a tool—it was part of him now, part of his identity. The burden it had carried, both physically and metaphorically, had been significant. Now, the emptiness left behind felt heavier than the bracer ever had, he felt hollow inside, absent of the power he had wielded. Even if only for a short time.

Leaning back in his high-backed chair, Rhyden steepled his fingers under his chin, his investigative eyes studying Kestus with a calculating gaze. The nobleman's calm demeanor unnerved him—how could someone be so composed after what they had been through? Rhyden had caused the deaths of dozens of men and women, just in the Seventh Star, and the Undercity was still burning because of his scheming. Yet, here he sat, untroubled as if discussing the weather.

"You have felt its power," Rhyden observed, his voice smooth, too smooth. Each word seemed to be measured, careful, as though there were deep gaps between every syllable. "Whatever you have seen, it is a minuscule piece of a much grander power. You found a truly rare thing."

Kestus frowned, his gaze moving from Rhyden to the bracer. "If you believe there is even more to the bracer than what I have already seen, you must know as well as I do...this object must be destroyed." The words came out harsh but Kestus didn't care, he needed to say them, needed his thoughts to be known. Kestus frowned deeper, his anger started to build. He meant every word, he had seen too much already and he resented this man. Power like this, unchecked, would destroy everything in its path.

He wanted me to steal the Shiftscape Bracer because he knows that the King could stomp him into the dust with its power. It can't be left in either of their possessions.

Rhyden's eyes darkened, his gaze drifting back to the bracer as if seeing something far beyond the physical. For a moment, Kestus could swear he saw a flicker of something ancient and terrible cross Rhyden's face, a shadow of something far older than the man before him.

"This is the key," Rhyden whispered. "A key to the Axis. To the Fractured Spine."

Leaning forward, this seemed like a straight answer, even if Kestus didn't understand what the man was talking about.

"What is the Axis?"

A bitter smile curled Rhyden's lips, his eyes gleaming with a mix of amusement and something even darker. "That is something too unbelievable to discuss right now. For now, little steps, Sir Kestus Retchet. You wouldn't understand... not yet. I believe you have seen something, it's just not enough to get you there. Not yet."

The ambiguity annoyed Kestus, still he bit back his frustration. "So what then? We do nothing? Let this thing sit here like some sort of cursed relic, while King Alikhan hunts for it? If this bracer is the key to something that dangerous, why not destroy it? Without the key, you can't open the lock."

"You are a thief, you know that is not true."

"The Undercity is burning. People are dying. And that's just because that bastard of a King doesn't have the Shiftscape Bracer. Tyven said you told him this will bring war and blood. Is this what you meant?"

Rhyden adjusted in his chair. "The Crimson Guard have returned from their seven year war against the Voy'Din. No, however, we will see worse things to come. The bracer is just one piece. Stealing it won't stop Alikhan's plans for long." Rhyden shook his head, his gaze hardening. "The Shiftscape Bracer cannot be destroyed, at least not by any means we possess. It will not be destroyed today or for many years to come. Right now we need to protect it from Alikhan, not eliminate it. This is the only tool we have that might give us a fighting chance."

Narrowing his eyes, Kestus was no fool. There was more Rhyden wasn't saying—there always was with these kinds of people. "I don't feel like I'm getting much information for how much you're talking."

A glimpse of amusement crossed Rhyden's face. "Patience, Sir Kestus. We are not yet to the end of the road. If you must hold onto something, hold onto this—I want you to wield the bracer." As if he were offering bread, Rhyden slid the artifact closer to Kestus. "You will be its protector, and in doing so, that will mean going forward we work together."

Kestus straightened, his eyes locking with Rhyden's. "Deal. Just don't think for a second I trust you."

Rhyden gave a small, dismissive wave of his hand. "I expect nothing less from a thief."

Silence fell between them as Kestus glanced towards Aegis, Rhyden's ironclad guard, like a statue he stood off to the side, dusting off a shelf as if the tension in the room didn't exist. "Tell me about your guardian? Why don't they take off the armor? And the Hushed. How were you both able to kill them? I saw them stand against several blades and nothing even cut their white fabrics."

"Aegis is… complicated. Know that he is a true friend. He helps me stay grounded. Aegis keeps me, the best version of myself. Without his aid, I would have gone mad" Rhyden's lips quirked into a half-smile. He rose from his chair with a fluid grace, crossing to the mantle where his sword rested. Taking it from its stand, he handed it to Kestus, hilt first. A pommel of a crescent moon with a dagger piercing it gleamed beneath the black leather that wrapped the grip. "This is *Des Roy*."

Fingers hesitant, Kestus grasped the hilt, and too his surprise, the cold metal could be felt through the leather. His hand brushed the etched glyphs, and as his thumb passed over the crystal orb embedded in the hilt, he felt a faint hum of energy. "This gem—it looks like the one in my dagger," Kestus remarked, noting the faint blue glow emanating from the orb. "Actually, up close the metal looks like the floor of the King's vault." The silver blade had veins of marble and gold, thin, but noticeable when near.

"The shard in your dagger, the bracer, and *Des Roy,* are indeed similar. This one is very different from yours though. I cannot control the Hushed with mine," Rhyden replied, his voice turning curious.

"You said the sword is like the floor in the vault? What do you mean?"

"Yeah, well the chamber leading to the vault. It was like a marble slab with silver and gold veins. Seeing the detail in the blade like this is incredible." Leaning closer, Kestus paused. "I want one."

"Fascinating. Everyone would think the treasure is in the vault, when really the most valuable thing is lying beneath their feet. Very clever." Rhyden mused, "Your dagger, may I see it?"

Leaning back, Kestus removed the stolen dagger from his belt and handed it to Rhyden. A deep confusion settled on Kestus' face. The sword began to feel different. Off.

"Hmm. You have no idea what this is, do you?" Rhyden smiled again, twisting the dagger in his hands, peering closely at the green shard in the hilt.

Kestus shook his head. The motion made him feel nauseous. A strange sound faintly teetered at the edge of his awareness. "I got it from King Alikhan's vault." His mouth felt dry.

"Indeed. Well, do not lose it." Rhyden handed the dagger back. "It is that shard that allows you to connect to your surroundings and control the Hushed."

The feeling of nausea suddenly went away, once

Kestus had his dagger in hand.

Kestus' eyes lingered on *Des Roy*.

Were you screaming? What was that?

"Alright. I think that is enough for today. I can see you are exhausted." Hand out, Rhyden asked for the sword back.

"Sure, but first, answer this at least. What are the Hushed?" Hands shaking, Kestus struggled to give Rhyden the sword.

"The Hushed are not of this world," Taking the weapon back and setting it gently on the mantle he returned to his chair. "Maybe they were part of your world before, however, now they exist in a place between realities. Phantoms of the Spine. A consequence of traveling through the gates or maybe a curse of the gods. I am not certain yet. As for how I am able to cut them, *Des Roy,* is forged from a rare ore. A metal that touches all realms of reality. It can pierce through anything, even the space between worlds."

"Can my dagger do that? Hurt them?"

Rhyden turned to Aegis. "In a matter of speaking. The power to control something offers a multiple of opportunities. As for the blade itself, no it can not. For now, get your rest. Our battle against King Alikhan is just beginning." He excused himself and walked to the archway before pausing, his silhouette framed by the spiral staircase beyond. Turning back, his gaze was sharp, almost a warning. "When you awake, you need to be ready to start training. Too much hangs in the balance for me to waste time explaining the secrets of our universe to a thief, if you go and get yourself killed."

And with that, Rhyden vanished into the shadows, leaving Kestus alone with the twisting turmoil of the uncertainty that lay ahead.

EPILOGUE
The King's Decree

King Alikhan stood in the grand hall of his castle, one hand resting on the pommel of the ceremonial sword strapped to his hip. The wound in his side, bandaged now, still ached and bled despite the stitches. Ignoring the pain, everything else was perfect, or it was until the Undercity rats scurried into his castle. His expression, illuminated by the oil lamp, was one of cold determination and a calm demeanor, a mask that hid the storm of rage and ambition brewing inside of his chest.

The vast chamber, once filled with nobles, courtiers, and advisors, was now nearly empty. Only a handful of royal blood, loyal guards, his daughter, and his advisor Doriunn Rethys, remained. The earlier meeting had sent the other lords scattering as soon as Alikhan had laid out his intentions, leaving those who stayed behind in tense silence.

Doriunn, a tall, gaunt figure cloaked in a royal black

and gold lined robe, stood at the King's side. The dark cloth he wore whispered against the bright stone floor, he was a shadowy presence that had lingered in the court for almost a decade now. Doriunn was the one who had whispered of the Axis, the cursed place between realms, and the ritual that could grant Alikhan his ultimate power.

With this knowledge, Alikhan had spent the past decade doing all he could to prepare every ritual and offering to ensure his dreams of power could become real. Then the Shiftscape Bracer—the key to that power—had slipped through the King's grasp, taken by Rhyden Tuo and the meddling Tyllieum Vendrick or the Blade, as he went by now.

Alikhan was not a man to be easily deterred however. The game had only just begun, and the final pieces were falling into place. Now his daughter and the Crimson Guard had returned, it wouldn't be long before he had the bracer back in hand. The fools who crossed him would only bring greater suffering upon themselves when this was over. Dutifully, Doriunn continued to encourage him that everything was still unfolding as planned, despite the delays.

Alikhan's gaze swept over his remaining audience, his dark eyes cold and filled with an even deeper darkness. These people didn't understand. They were loyal to him not out of love but out of fear.

They shifted uneasily, their expressions veiled. Alikhan wondered who would be the first to speak —to challenge him.

None dared.

The King's voice cut through the silence like an axe. "The Undercity has defied me for the last time." His words echoed off the stone walls, heavy and clear. "For too long,these gangs have been operating in the shadows. Growing bolder and bolder, thinking they could escape my rule. My wrath. They have harbored criminals, thieves, and traitors. Starstride, RavenHood—they are no longer gangs to be tolerated. They are enemies of the people and of the crown!"

"None stand against the crown!" Screamed Captain RosenThorn raising her sword in salute to her father.

"None shall." Alikhan smiled at his daughter.

Then unable to contain the rage inside, his smile faded as he began to pace, his boots striking the floor. "The time for leniency has passed. I will not allow the Undercity—or anyone within Tare'Envel or beyond—to challenge my authority. I have led our Kingdom to prosperity and have elevated this rule higher than any before me! Yet, they spread falsehoods about me and call me Alikhan the Stern. Every member of Starstride, RavenHood, or anyone that dares defy me will be hunted down and eradicated. The rose has bloomed and with its beauty comes its thorns."

The nobles remained silent and still, too afraid even to breathe.

Captain RosenThorn scanned the crowd, ready to pounce on anyone who spoke against her father. Their faces were pale as the King's decree sank in. Alikhan's eyes flickered toward his advisor Doriunn, whose expression was unreadable beneath his hood, however, an almost imperceptible nod from the man vindicated Alikhan.

Blood would spill across Tare'Envel.

Walking to his window, Alikhan peered out at his kingdom. The High City was glittering against the darkening sky, the wealth and opulence of his realm laid out before him like a crown of jewels. Beyond the lights, deep in the cess-pool of the Undercity, a different world existed. A world of shadow, of rebellion, of those who thought they could defy him.

"Not for long!" The King growled between gritted teeth.

The Undercity had long been a blade in his side, a festering pit of lawlessness and insubordination. It was time to cut the cancer out, once and for all.

More than that, the Undercity would serve another purpose. The blood of its people, the criminals, the dissidents, the gangs—they would all die for something far greater than themselves. They would die for his rise, his calling, his godhood.

The very thought of it sent a surge of anticipation through the King. For years, Alikhan had ruled with a firm hand, it was the only way to push the world forward, growth came from struggle. People had a terrible habit of getting stuck in the mundane, they lacked imagination and innovation. He had always been bound by the limits of his own mortality, of the constraints of this world. Until now, with the Axis—if what Doriunn had spoken of was true— it would change everything. The fractured spine between worlds was a pathway to unimaginable power, and with the Bloodied Vessel awakened, that power would be his to command.

"Doriunn." Alikhan called without turning, his gaze still fixed on his Tare'Envel. "The time for the Goddess' return is near, yes?"

"Yes." Doriunn bowed. Their voices not loud enough for anyone else to hear.

Despite it being what he wanted to know, Alikhan was unsatisfied.

"How near!?"

Doriunn moved to stand beside the King, his approach silent as death. "Soon, my Lord King. The ritual will be ready in a matter of days. The gate is almost complete. All that remains is the final preparation—the blood must be offered, the sacrifices made. Once that is done, the gate will open, and godhood will be yours."

Days. Alikhan smiled to himself and took a deep breath. He could wait that long.

"And you're certain that the bracer isn't necessary? That Rhyden and the thief don't matter?"

"The Shiftscape Bracer is merely one part of the puzzle." Doriunn replied calmly, his words almost rehearsed as if he had said this several times before. "It's power is significant, yes. However, it is not the only way to achieve our goal. Rhyden and the thief are delays. Nothing more. With your daughter here and the forces she has gathered, they stand no chance. Their efforts will be in vain. None will be able to prevent your new path."

Alikhan finally turned to face Doriunn, his eyes gleaming with passion. "Good." With a toothy grin, Alikhan let out a small laugh. "I want Rhyden's head. He stole from me. He defied me. And no one defies the King."

The advisor inclined his head. "As you wish, my Lord King. By the time the ritual is complete, there will be no one left to oppose you."

Alikhan nodded, satisfied. "Captain RosenThorn, gather your Crimson Guard," he commanded, speaking louder and gesturing his daughter forward. "I want them patrolling the streets of the Undercity by sunrise. Arrest anyone who look like they belong to a gang, anyone who speaks against me, or anyone who even breathes a word of rebellion. I want the Undercity purged."

Captain RosenThorn bowed. "It will be done, my King."

Alikhan watched as Doriunn, with a gesture toward the door, departed with his daughter, the advisor's robes trailing behind him like a wisp of smoke and her armor scraping the ground like a blade. The King's mind was already racing ahead, plotting out every move, every order. The Crimson Guard would sweep through the Undercity, crushing Starstride and RavenHood beneath their iron boots. The blood would flow, and with it, his path to power would be paved.

Alikhan could already feel new strength thrumming in his veins, just beyond his reach.

"Soon. Oh so very soon." He whispered to himself.

Turning back to the window, Alikhan allowed himself a moment of satisfaction. He had ruled Tare'Envel for many years, and now, with the Axis at his fingertips and the goddess stirring in her slumber, his rule would soon become eternal.